Amber's Grace

By Dana Bowen and Chloe Brogan

Thank you to my husband Brock for vulnerably sharing and advising on the experience of being nuerodivergent and in love.

Chloe Brogan

I can't think of a real dedication. I think, for me, this book is dedicated to everyone who sees themselves or their loved ones in the pages. This book has my whole heart wrapped up inside of it. For everyone reading this, I hope you see the beauty, complexity, and love inside the story.

Dana Bowen

TRIGGER WARNINGS
Reference to Domestic Abuse
Reference to Threats of Violence
Pregnancy Complications
Reference to Cheating
Sexual Content

TABLE OF CONTENTS

Chapter One

"Yeah, I am literally parked out front. Order me a lemon drop. I'm only late because I had to help Mr. Broody-pants... Well, don't ask me why Saul isn't fired, ask Nathan... Alright, I'm coming in." I tap my phone to hang up. I stand outside of Cici's bar; a whole lot has changed over this year, but Cici's has remained. The neon purple sign above may be new, but I know when I walk in it will all still be the same faces.

I open the door and the little bell tings above me. The place is packed, but Nathan and Catherine have already claimed 'our table'. Catherine moved out of my apartment and in with Nathan a month or so after his dad's funeral. I'm not going to lie. That was hard on me. I am an extrovert with social anxiety, losing my in-house best friend sucked. I also was worried she was rushing things. Nathan is my boss and my longtime good friend. Catherine is my best friend. Their first unofficial break up was bad enough doing it again would suck. Here we are, though, seven months later and they are stronger than ever. Which is great. Now I only have one problem; Mr. Broody-pants at work.

Nathan doesn't always join us on Saturdays. I actually like it when he does. I know it's crazy being out with a couple when you're single, but they've never made me feel like a third wheel. I maneuver the obstacles of drunk college kids to get to our table. Nathan stands as I reach the table and pulls me into a quick hug before giving up the seat next to Catherine.

Last year I had to watch Nathan wither away into nothing after his dad died. I don't mean that literally because he's a massive mountain of a man. Even at his weakest, I'd still bet on him in a fight. I mean, Nathan became a shell. I watched his eyes fade, and his shoulders hunch further and further.

Now, he looks like himself again. He still has his long hair, but it's almost always pulled into a sleek man bun. Meghan helps him take care of it and even shapes his beard for him. It's shorter now and looks intentional. The best part is how happy he looks. His eyes have smile lines around them again, and his brows are relaxed to a normal place on his face. It all multiplies tenfold when he looks at Catherine. I can only hope to find someone who looks at me with half that admiration.

Catherine throws her arms around me. "Amber! I've missed you!"

I hug her back and giggle. "I missed you too."

"You both literally had lunch two days ago." Nathan sighs and shakes his head.

"TWO DAYS TOO LONG!" Catherine exclaims, which wins her a chuckle from Nathan. Catherine turns back, pushing a light yellow drink toward me. "So, tell me what's up with Mr. Broodypants."

I sigh dramatically and down half of the drink in my glass, which I regret instantly. "Well," I look pointedly at Nathan, pound on my chest and burp. "Saul pushed a security update through on the main computer."

"There weren't any security updates," Nathan says while looking at his phone. When I don't speak again, Nathan looks up. "Fuuuuck, what was it?"

"An update virus. The fucker was really hard to remove." I say. "We ended up calling half of the University's IT department, and do you know who ended up fixing it?" I pause for dramatic effect. "SOME TWELVE-YEAR-OLD!"

"Twelve?" Catherine asks.

"Well, not twelve, but I don't think he can even grow a beard yet. Some students overheard me yelling at IT for not prioritizing the issue and he helped me. Do you have any idea how embarrassing it is to be shown up in front of a fully filled library? BY A CHILD?"

Nathan sighs. "I'm sorry that happened."

"Sorry? Maybe if you didn't ignore his calls, I wouldn't have to do it! Why are we still keeping him around?" I dramatically roll my eyes.

"I mean, the front computers and checking books aren't even his job. He's there to help the students find what they need, and reserve study rooms, and wheel projectors around. He's GRACIOUSLY giving us each one night off." Nathan looks at me pointedly, and I wonder for the hundredth time why nothing Saul ever does actually makes him mad. He's never specifically upset with him, and I think I've only ever witnessed mild annoyance twice. It's ridiculous. The man is unflappable.

"I know, I know, I just don't understand why when I say, 'don't touch anything I did it all', he still does. He is so technologically delayed, how does he make it in the modern world?" I roll my eyes and finish my drink, waving to Charles. He smiles as he approaches the table.

"Hello my loves, hey Nathan." His soft British accent is instantly soothing.

"Hi Charles, I feel like I haven't seen you in forever!" I saw him last Saturday but I grew use to him and Cici coming to my apartment to have dinner with us. Well with Catherine, when she moved out I lost out on the free family dinners. I'd still like to think they've scooped me up as an adopted niece.

He pinches my cheek affectionately and winks at Catherine. "I'm always here, love. What can I get you all? Another round of the same things?"

"Please!" Catherine and I say at the same time. We both laugh and the crows' feet around Charles's eyes deepen.

"I'll be back in a moment, then." Charles weaves his way back toward the bar. Every so often, the door behind me will open, letting in a gush of warm summer air. I love the feel of the warm summer nights, and tonight feels exceptionally peaceful. My friends are here, and we are all finally settling into a happy routine.

"So, are we done being mad at Nathan and Saul?" Nathan asks.

"I guess... for now. For the record, though, I'm never really mad at you." I smile and he smiles back, but that smile disappears immediately.

"What's wrong? Do I have something in my teeth?" I impusively rub my index finger agrresively across my front teeth.

"Uh," Nathan stutters and clears his throat. "Uh, don't turn around right now, okay?"

"Why?" I look past Nathan to where Charles has slowed down, still holding our drinks. "What's going on?"

"Nathan, what's happening?" Catherine leans forward, trying to look over my shoulder as Charles deposits the drinks on the table.

"Do you want me to distract them so that you can sneak out the back?" Charles asks.

"Sneak out the back? Who is here?" I look between Nathan and Charles, fear climbing up my throat. I still haven't looked, but given the way Nathan is eyeing whoever is giving me the creeps.

Nathan looks like he's going to speak again, but nothing comes out of his mouth.

"Wow, I didn't expect to see you here." An uncomfortably familiar voice wraps around my neck and strangles me.

Suddenly, I can't look away from Nathan's face. My brain short circuits. I close my eyes as a raging tornado of old emotions surges up my throat. I hear Nathan say something that I can't decipher around the sound of my heart attempting to break free of my ribs.

"Hey Amber, it's been a while." The masculine voice topped with annoyance for not originally responding sends me over the edge.

I'm standing before I even realize it. "You've got to be absolutely fucking kidding me." I spit. He is the last person I ever wanted to see again. I hate Andrew Fucking Brinks; son of the Bethton Groves Police Chief, top of his class at Bethton Grove University, and my ex-fiance.

Then my eyes meet the second person I ever wanted to see again. My sister's stunned face stares back at me, and her husband looks perplexed, but there's a menacing glint in his eyes that unsettles me. I haven't seen Brittany or Andrew in at least four years. My sister still looks like a younger, prettier version of me. Her hair is braided over her shoulder, almost silvery blonde in the poor bar lighting. Her eyes are practically bugging out of her skull like a deer in headlights. I would assume my outburst wasn't the reaction she was expecting.

Andrew looms behind Brittany. He seems to share my disgust and irritation with the situation, looking at me like he would rather be anywhere else rather than here in the bar. His hand rests possesively on Brittany's shoulder. He appears to be tense and ready to throw her behind himself if necessary. The thought makes a laugh bubble up from my stomach. It sounds insane when it bursts from me.

"Amber–" Brittany starts to speak.

I hold up a hand, silencing my sister. The sound of her voice feels like a punch to the gut. "Listen, I've already had an annoying and stressful evening."

"Amber, just listen." Andrew tries to cut in, his tone is gruff and annoyed

"No, no, I don't think I want to hear anything you have to say." I glare up at him. "Particularly, YOU."

Then Catherine is beside me. She takes my hand reassuringly but says nothing. I squeeze her hand to remind myself where I am. "It's great that you guys are here–actually, that's a lie. I was really really hoping to never see your faces again. SO, have a delightful visit, and fuck back off to Florida as soon as possible." I turn to Catherine, who starts pulling me away from everyone, toward the bathroom.

"Wait, Amber." Andrew's hand grasps my forearm tight enough that it might bruise. My stomach churns at the touch. "We aren't going back to Florida, we just closed on a house by–"

I think I'm having a PTSD attack or war flashbacks or maybe it's déjà vu; the next thing I know, Andrew is staggering back, catching a chair for support as the sound of my palm connecting with his face shatters the surrounding air. Brittany flinches hard, stepping out of the way.

"I could have sworn the last time I saw you, I told you not to fucking touch me. Apparently, you didn't learn." Anger boils my blood. I pride myself on being reasonably level-headed and I try not to cuss when possible. My mother always told me cussing was for people without extensive vocabulary. While I don't normally listen to things my mother says, I guess the ideology stuck. I find words stuck in my mouth sometimes while I look for something to say. But I guess tonight is an exception.

Catherine grabs my shoulders and spins me almost violently away from the scene unfolding. "Amber, I think you made your point," she whispers. "Let's take a walk."

The entire bar is silent and I feel like I'm coming out of a bubble. The silence slams into me as it feels like I make eye contact with everyone in the bar. Fights aren't rare. This is a college bar, but I feel the weight of what it's like to be the center of attention. I look back over my shoulder. Nathan has a hand on Andrew's chest while Andrew stares murderously between the big man and me.

Brittany seems to have collapsed in a puddle of tears against Charles. The poor man looks pained, like he doesn't know if he should comfort her or not. His kindness wins out in the end as he sets a hand on her back. I can't be too upset with him because after all these years, I know he's never been unkind in his life. But then the entire scene disappears behind the swinging bathroom door and my brain goes silent.

"Alright, let's breathe. What's happening?" Catherine raises a hand as a signal to stop.

I take a deep breath. "Okay, so that's my sister and my ex, and they shouldn't be here. Why are they here? It doesn't make sense. THEY LIVE IN FLORIDA AND IT'S NOT EVEN A DAMN HOLIDAY!" the words fall out of my mouth at top speed. I feel ready to combust as my arms swing wide.

"Okay, let's tone down the aggressive gesturing," Catherine says in a soothing voice, and I lower my hands. "Remember, they said they moved here."

"WHAT!" I stomp my foot like an angry toddler. I can't help it and clench my hands and let out a cry of fury.

The door cracks open an inch behind Catherine. "Are you okay?" Nathan whisper-yells into the bathroom.

"NO!" I yell, turning in circles, frantically wanting to hit something or throw something. I can't even come close to actually expressing the TNT-level explosive emotions inside of me.

Part of me feels like I'm watching myself from outside of my body. I feel like some part of me watching my reaction knows I'm being unreasonable, but the part of me that still hurts doesn't care. I have carefully constructed the life I have now, and I refuse to let them derail me again. It took way too long to heal last time, my body and mind can't handle another assault.

Nathan pushes the door to the women's bathroom and walks inside, locking it behind himself. He's got Catherine's cheetah print purse in his left hand, and my unicorn messenger bag on his shoulder. The sight would normally throw me into a fit of laughter so violent I'd choke. But not even that cheers me up. When he turns around, his eyes are downcast, like he's embarrassed to be in here. My heart jumps a little at the kindness of my friends. But it's too small to change the course of fury and pain sizzling beneath my skin.

"Can I do anything for you?" He asks quietly. We share a look, and I can see him absorbing everything going through me. I am reminded of the way he took care of me during the first year after Andrew and I broke up. The many times he sat with me while I cried over the betrayal the first time around. I remember the days spent in his office while I would fume and rage over my mother's reactions to the situations and the gentle support he offered through my parents following divorce.

"Put a hit out on them." I deadpan.

He nods and pulls out his phone, pretending to make a call. "Hi, I'd like to place a hit on someone." He is quiet and nods for a few seconds. "Yes... yes... dismembered preferably."

A sad-sounding giggle bubbles out of me, and I realize I'm crying. Catherine wraps her arms around me, hugging me tightly. I cling to her like a child, leaning in for even more support.

"They can't be here, they just can't." Tears fall nonstop. "They ruined everything. My parents literally divorced because of them, and I haven't talked to my mom since. It's been four years. This is some fucked up joke. I lost my whole family. The universe is laughing at me." A sob tears through my throat and cut off anything else I was going to say.

I feel Nathan's hand rest on my shoulder. "You may have lost one 'family', but you built something way better. We're here and we are your family. The universe isn't mocking you, it's just a reminder that this–" Nathan gestures around us. "–is your family. Charles, Cici, Larry, Mariposa, Yuri, me, Catherine, and everyone else are here to love and support you. Fuck them. You have more than they will ever have."

I lean into Nathan as well, he and Catherine stay close, arms wrapped around me. "I don't deserve you guys." I blubber. I doubt they even under-stand through the snot and tears. "I don't know what I would have done if you guys hadn't been here tonight."

Neither of them let go until I have composed myself and reach for a paper towel to wipe my face. I look over Catherine's shoulder to see myself in the mirror. I look like hell. Black runs down my face, and my makeup looks similar to the raccoon eyes that were popular in two-thou-sand and seven. I look like the younger version of myself who just crawled out of a mosh pit at a Twenty-One Pilots concert.

"Do you want to go home?" Catherine asks.

"I don't know." I grumble.

"Is it okay if we leave the bathroom and decide?" Nathan says.

Catherine gives him a sympathetic smile and I nod. He practically runs from the bathroom. Well, 'runs' in the way you'd expect a massive mountain of a man to run and still keep his dignity.

Nathan leans back in and waves us on. "Coast is clear, I think they left."

"Wanna get smashed and go back to my place and watch The Office?" Catherine nudges me forward.

"Damn straight I do." We both head through the door and go to the bar.

"Well, isn't it the boxing champ? Can I offer you some free pickle backs to celebrate?" Larry laughs and starts pouring the tequila in shot glasses while Charles pours some pickle juice.

The bar is busier than I remembered it being as we crowd at the end of the bar under the TV closest to the bathrooms. People seem to do me a kindness and they all try not to stare, but now and then someone points and whispers to their neighbor. Thankfully, I don't see anyone that knows my mom, or anyone that knows me. It's mostly college students. Maybe if any of them see me around the library, they will be nicer when the computers run slowly. For all they know, I am an unhinged psycho. I smile to myself at the thought.

Charles gives me a sympathetic smile, sliding the half-filled shot glass of pickle juice across the table. "I really hope I never piss you off, love. You have a scary arm on you."

I attempt a smile, and I think he knows I don't have much energy. As soon as my shot glass is empty, Larry is refilling it.

"It was incredible." Larry says like he's awestruck. "I would pay big money to watch it again."

I laugh weakly, "well, they said they're moving here, so who knows?" I shrug, "Maybe you'll see a round two." I seriously hope not, but I don't think I'll get that lucky. Something about the encounter sours my stomach. Why would they just randomly show up here? Were they looking for me specifically?

Larry gives me a third free shot, and my skin glows warmer and warmer. I know Nathan buys another round of lemon drops, and

Catherine talks to Larry about work tomorrow night. I can't hear much of the conversation. My sister's face is plastered across my mind's eye. The way she looked at me when I stood up. Her eyes after I swung on Andrew...

Fuck, I hate all of this already. I feel emotion still simmering under my skin. I didn't like the way she flinched away, even though I'm still mad at her, something felt extremely off between all of us that stems deeper than just the confrontation. I don't know what it is, but call it sister instinct. Apparently, that never really goes away. There was a small sliver of time, right when Brittany started college, where I was excited for us to become closer. I thought getting away from mom would do wonders for her like it did for me. But then that entire year was bombed when she started acting weird and well, sleeping with my fiance. I hate thinking about it so much.

Catherine and I walk out of the bar sometime later, arm in arm. Nathan trails behind us, still holding the bags. The last thing I remember is sitting on the floor of Catherine's living room, drunkenly laughing as Jim pranks Dwight again.

Chapter Two

"Good morning Ladies." Nathan sing songs as he prances into the living room.

"Shut the fuck up." Catherine grumbles from the sofa.

"This is why I don't drink." Nathan laughs.

"I thought it was because your dad died from being an alcoholic." Catherine rolls over and glares at him.

Nathan rolls his eyes. "Do you guys want coffee or not?"

"Yes, please." We say in unison.

I slide myself from the sofa onto the white shag area carpet in their apartment. My head feels too heavy for my neck as I lay lifelessly on the floor staring at the ceiling. When I'm sure I will not puke, I sit up, still in the same clothes I had on yesterday. I check my pockets and find my phone. There are three missed calls from my parents.

"What? Why did my parents call me?" I haven't spoken to them in years. Well, my mom, at least. Every now and then, my dad calls me from Ohio to be sure that I am still alive. Usually those phone calls end up with him venting about something mom said in an email or some new conspiracy theory he heard in a podcast.

"I told Nathan we should've taken your phone..." Catherine looks at her fingers, fidgeting.

"Why? What do you mean... Oh god..." I try to pull from my hazy memories what happened but I can't.

"You called your parents last night and left a very, uh, spicy voicemail for each of them." Nathan says, trying not to spill two full mugs of coffee. He's already dressed for the day, hair down and wet, which is unusual. Not the wet part, but I almost never see it down.

"What! What did I say?" I feel like puking all over again. I'm not sure if it's from the hangover or the fact I called the mother I completely cut out of my life.

"I don't know. I was just as wasted as you were. You'd have to ask Nathan." Catherine sighs, covering her eyes.

"Nathan," I say sternly.

"Yes?" He says in a fearful voice. He lowers a steaming mug of coffee to me, not making eye contact. It feels like an offering. But I don't know if it's an offering of more support, or an offering like an apology. I take the scalding cup between my hands and lean over the mug so that the steam coats my cheeks before I take my first sip. It burns a trail all the way to my stomach and incrementally settles the pounding in my brain.

"What did I say?" I narrow my gaze on Nathan, knowing he will break first..

Nathan looks at Catherine for help, but she doesn't uncover her eyes. He sets her coffee down on the end table and crosses his arms over his chest.

"Do I have to repeat it?" I respond with a glare, so he knows if he doesn't tell me, he will only have a few minutes to live. "Fine." He clears his throat, pulls out his phone, and adorns as high of a pitch the goliath of a man can manage.

"Hi MOOM! What the fuck? What the fuck gives you people the fucking right to fucking exist? How dare you let Brittany within one thousand miles of me? ANY of you could have called me to give me a heads up. BUT NO! I bet you pieces of butt set us up. You guys wanted her to ambush me! You always pick her side!" His voice cracks andNathan slides his phone back to his pocket. Then he does a little bow. "I think there may have been a few extra curse words or other things mixed in, but that's the basic idea."

"Are you kidding me?" I shout.

"Nope." Nathan deadpans, and Catherine shakes her head. Her hands are still over her eyes.

"Fuck..."

"I'm sure it's fine." Catherine looks at me.

I start the first voicemail from my mom and put it on speaker.

"Amber... Honey, just got your message. Sweetie, Brittany said you hit Andrew? Again? Was that really necessary? It's been years honey, you need to let this go. It's getting childish. I didn't tell you because I assumed this would be your reaction. And it's not like you'd have picked up the phone, anyway. So I didn't see the point. Call me back, and you owe your sister an apology."

I set the phone on the table and play the next message from my dad.

"Are you okay? Since when do you call me when you're drunk? I had to call your bitch of a mother to even find out what's going on. I don't know what has happened over the last few years. You are such a good kid. Now, look at you, acting like a drunk mess. Do you want me to come out? Anyway, I'm sorry that your mom and sister ambushed you like that. Seems like something your mother would do. Next time, right hook, closed fist. Really knock him down a peg. Slapping is for petty girls and children. Break Andrew's fucking nose. If I see him before you, I'll make sure to get him good. Ugh, your sister is calling me now. Love you."

I play the third one from my mom.

"Your father just called me furious. Honey... Why would you poke the bear like that? He already doesn't like that your sister is here and thinks this is all my fault. Now he wants us to all sit down and have dinner. He made it sound like he wants to come back from Ohio to chat. He's going to need somewhere to stay. Can he sleep at your house? He sure as heck isn't staying with me and you shouldn't make him stay at a hotel. Apparently, he thinks you need an intervention. I can't disagree that your drinking is obviously out of control. You attacked an innocent man in a drunken stupor. Sweetie, you really should call your sister. Your father called her as well, and she's devastated. I don't know what's gotten into you. Your sister deserves better. She and Andrew have done nothing wrong." My moms gaslighting shrill voice finally stops.

"Wow... They sound angry." Catherine sat up while listening and now holds her own steaming cup of coffee.

"Thanks, Catherine. I wasn't sure." I hear the bite in my tone and clear my throat before apologizing. "Sorry, that was rude."

"At least your dad doesn't seem too pissed," Nathan says. "If anything, he seems to be on your side."

"That's only because everything my mom does pisses him off. AND everything I do pisses her off. He would let me get away with murder if he thought it would make Mom mad." I lay back down on the floor, throwing my arms over my face. "What am I going to do?"

"I don't know, Amber... But whatever happens, we are here for you." Catherine pats my shoulder.

Nathan's alarm on his watch goes off and I jump. "I gotta go to work for a few hours today..." There's a pause and I look up to find him watching me warily. "You can take the day off if you need to." He says mildly.

"No, no, no. I can't just sit alone with my thoughts all day." I know my thoughts, they'll drown me if I let them.

"You could stay here with me until I have to go into the bar tonight." Catherine offers.

"I refuse to let them ruin anything for me. The best thing I can do is just go back to life as normal. They don't matter. This doesn't mean anything. It's been years." I don't know if I'm convincing them or myself. "Everything is perfectly fine. I got all of my emotions out last night."

Nathan and Catherine share a look that makes it seem like they don't quite believe me. After a second though, Nathan nods and heads back toward the bedroom he and Catherine share.

"I guess I need to head home to take a shower." I take a few big gulps of my coffee.

"Don't rush. Take the coffee with you and just bring the mug back later." She smiles and wraps me in a tight hug. "I know this is stressful. But I love you, and I'm here, no matter what." She gives me another reassuring squeeze before walking me to the front door.

Coffee mug in hand, I walk down the few steps from the townhouse door to the street and head across the parking lot. Holding the coffee mug in one hand, I dig through my bag for my keys. I find them and unlock the door. As I head inside, I see Catherine standing across the parking lot, waving from her front door. I wave back and lock the door behind me.

When Catherine moved out, she and Nathan lived above The Grove for a month or so until a townhouse became available. I don't know that Nathan was super thrilled that it was directly across the parking lot from me, but it's the only thing that keeps me sane. Bethton Grove is a small town. There aren't many people who don't know your business, and there aren't many people that are friend material. I've long outgrown the party scene, so campus isn't really an option, and the kids are practically babies, anyway. Everyone else is busy, crazy, married with kids, or old. When Mariposa moved away, I was basically alone. Catherine has been my first genuine friend in years. We run back and forth to talk to each other whenever we want. Half of the week we spend eating dinner with each other.

I stare into my empty apartment and run my hand over my face. I am exhausted. I have lived a happy, drama-free life since I cut off my mother and sister. My mother always takes Brittany's side and my father always takes mine. The older I get, though, it seems as if my father only takes my side to drive my mother crazy. It's been a constant war my entire childhood into my adult life. Brittany and I pitted against each other. Then when Andrew cheated on me, my dad took my side and mom took hers and that was the last straw for them. They divorced shortly after. They wanted to put me in the middle since Brittany was in Florida, so I just stepped away and stopped talking to my mother. Dad only calls on important holidays and birthdays. My dad was horrible to mom but as an adult I see she was just as viscous to him. Passive aggressively hiding his stuff, making him feel crazy. Then he would explode and scream horrible things. That always devolved into a fight that made my father into a villain and my mother some sort of martyr.

I slide off my shoes and set them next to the door. I start my way to the shower. Maybe some warm water will settle my thoughts. No one will reach out to me again after last night, which would be amazing. I open my bathroom door and turn on the shower to high heat to get a nice steam going. I shimmy out of the jeans and shirt I wore to the bar last night. Catching myself in the mirror, I run my fingers along my petite frame. I wish I could put on a little weight. Maybe I'd at least have b cups. I have my dad's body–perpetually boney. It's a stupid thing to complain about, at least that's what my mother always said. I just try not to look too closely and stay as positive as possible. If I just pretend I don't have a body, then it won't matter. Bodies are just made for clothes, anyway. If I pick clothes that make me happy, what's underneath doesn't feel like such a big deal.

I slide into the scalding hot water to burn whatever is left of this hangover off of me. My skin turns pink from the heat. As I shampoo my hair, my mind wanders. What if they keep bothering me? What if this is some sort of sick prank? Why would they even move back here? I just need to keep moving. My mind is only doing this because I'm not doing anything. I rinse out my hair, finish cleaning up, and hop out of the shower. I dry off with the butterfly towel Catherine gave me. It's a children's towel, but she said it reminded her of me, so it's my favorite.

I hang the towel up and walk buck-naked through my living room. A perk of living alone is that I can be naked whenever I want. I go into my room and pick out a bright mustard yellow dress and black leggings. Maybe if I dress happy I'll feel happy. Act normal and things will be normal. I live by the saying "Fake it till ya make it." I throw my hair up into a blonde messy bun and head my ass out the door.

I'm already going to be a minute late, but it's fine. Until I realize I left my car parked by Cici's last night. I look across the parking lot and Nathan has already left.

"FUCK!" I startle an old lady walking her Yorkie when I scream.

"That's not a word for nice young ladies..." the woman mumbles under her breath. The stupid dog yips and barks the entire way past me and I have an urge to bark back. But I don't need my day getting any worse. So I shoulder my unicorn messenger bag, flip the bird at my side and start my stupid walk to work.

Chapter Three

As soon as I cross the street heading toward campus, a small rumble of thunder shakes the clouds in the distance. I pick up my pace, zigzagging through paths and making a beeline for the library as fast as I can. It's early on Saturday morning, so the campus is like a ghost town, napkin tumbleweeds and all. There's another crack of thunder; way closer than before, and now I'm practically running. I can see the library across the massive courtyard,the massive lions guarding the front doors of the library. They stare me down, daring me to make it in time. Sometimes I think when no one is looking they have to talk to each other. I wonder what they'd say about me right now? Would they cheer me on or laugh at my probable failure?

Thirty seconds and I'll be there. I can make it.

One massive raindrop blinds my left eye.

Twenty seconds.

I beeline around the weird decorative bushes in the middle of the way.

I'm so close.

BOOM.

The rain crashes into me, similar to how the shower hit my skin this morning. An absolute storm whips through my clothes and hair. I run as quickly as I can up the stairs and through the big double doors. Air conditioning slams me in the face like a wall of ice. It's empty inside, thankfully. It feels like the storm-clouds follow me inside, as my dislike for the day rolls off me.

I speed walk around the front desk and stow my dripping bag underneath. I grab a handful of napkins from a drawer and start dabbing at my face, neck, and hair. I'm thankful I didn't wear makeup today or it would be dripping down my face. This has to be some sort of cosmic joke. It can't already be this bad of a day. I pull my hair out of the messy bun, flinging water everywhere as I attempt to ring out the ends into the trash can by the desk.

"Hey, guess it's raining a bit hard today." A timid voice taps my shoulder.

I jump so hard I bang my knee on the knobs of the filing cabinet stuffed under the desk.

"What the fuck, Saul?" I whirl on him without even thinking and practically topple to the floor as my rolling chair tips dangerously to the left. My hair arcs out wildly, slapping me in the face as my arms flail out in a futile attempt to steady myself. Saul grabs the arm to right it so I don't fall flat on my face.

"Sorry, I didn't mean to scare–"

"DUDE, if you didn't want to scare me, you shouldn't have walked up behind me so quietly!" My voice cracks when I say dude like a twelve year old boy.

"I didn't realize I was being quiet. Are you okay?" Saul asks in his stupid, quiet voice.

"I don't know, Saul; do I look OKAY?" I gesture up and down my soaked clothes.

At least he's smart enough to stay quiet, but his eyes travel the length of my body before sweeping over my face without actually looking me in the eye.

"No, I'm not okay. I was thirty seconds away from the door when a fucking MONSOON hit! I have a HORRIBLE hangover. My dad thinks I'm an alcoholic; I shouldn't even care, I'm an adult but he's my dad. I got blackout drunk last night and called my mom and him. They're both pissed, and I haven't even talked to MOM in years. AND ALL OF THAT WAS AFTER I WAS LATE TO DRINKS LAST NIGHT BECAUSE I WAS HELPING YOU DO SHIT AND MY SISTER AND EX-FIANCE SHOWED UP AT THE BAR TO LET ME KNOW THEY'RE FUCKING MOVING BACK HERE AND I SLAPPED MY EX BECAUSE HE STILL HASN'T LEARNED TO KEEP HIS HANDS OFF OF ME." I gasp in a breath. I didn't realize I wasn't breathing or how loud I was until I hear my words echo around the empty building.

Saul hasn't moved. His arms are hanging lamely at his sides, and I want to punch his perfectly neutral face. His outfit reminds me of oatmeal, annoyingly plain and monochromatic. Except for the neon orange diving watch he insists on wearing constantly. I asked him about it once and his only response was, 'It's practical.' What a dweeb.

"It just all feels like some sort of fucked up cosmic joke in a shitty sitcom..." I feel tears start rolling down my face.

"Do you need a hug?" Saul says quietly. He still hasn't actually moved, and I can't quite seem to catch his eye. It's like he's staring at my nose or my forehead or something and it bothers me. I want him to look me in the eye and shrivel up under the laser beams I'm sure will shoot out at any second.

"I don't know," I answer honestly. I don't remember standing, but I take a hesitant step forward, and as if he can read my mind. Saul takes the last three steps toward me and wraps his arms around me. For a second, it feels stiff and awkward. I'm uncomfortably aware of my soaked clothes and my dripping hair that's plastered on my back. I take a deep breath, assuming that he's going to let go. He doesn't though, he actually tightens his grip on me a bit more and when I exhale, my entire body seems to fuse with his. I wrap my arms around him and hold on. The tears that were falling a moment ago have calmed; in their place, I attempt steadying breaths.

Saul isn't a big guy. He's staggeringly average, almost painfully so. He's tall-ish, and he doesn't appear very muscular. He doesn't have any particularly interesting features. Wait, but he smells good, and his sweater vest is soft against my cheek. His hair is a deep red, and hangs across his forehead in that ugly-swishy-bieber-style that was super popular with middle schoolers ten years ago.

His cheek rests gently against my forehead, and I focus on the sound of his breath in his chest to help calm myself down. I don't know how long we stand like that, but it feels like I'm shaken from a daze. I realize I still haven't let go, and heat rushes to my face as I finally pull away. His cheeks are slightly pink too, and he's looking at me in this curious way, like he's seeing me for the first time. I think my face has a similar expression.

"Sorry," I say, wrapping my arms around myself, suddenly chilled. My hair feels heavy and tangled and I put it back up just so I have a reason to move.

"For?" He looks genuinely perplexed.

"For... holding you hostage, I think." My smile is flat and umcomfortable.

Saul looks like he's going to say something, but Nathan clears his throat off to the right of us and I cringe.

"We need to talk." Nathan looks angry. Well I'm sure angry is the right word. More of like a dad who caught their kid smoking.

"I don't know what I did, but I'm sorry." Saul says in a sheepish voice. Saul is a good three inches shorter than Nathan's six foot and six inches. Nathan could flatten him if he wanted.

"No, not you, Saul. Can you excuse us?" Nathan says in an uncom-fortably professional tone.

"Uh, yes, sir." Saul scurries away from us.

"Amber, I love you. You know that, right?" Nathan says, placing his hand on my shoulder.

"Yes, although I'm not too confident in that at this moment." I try to joke but my half ass smirk falls flat.

"Wonderful. I'm going to need you to take some time off." He has a far too toothy smile on his face, but frustration in his eyes.

"What? Why?" I haven't done anything wrong.

"You just screamed at a fellow employee. While I am your friend, I also am your boss. If Saul wasn't the pushover he was, I'd be getting a call from H.R." He sighs, "If you won't willingly take time off, I'll have to make you. You aren't okay, no matter what you claim. I can't have you losing control of yourself on students or Saul in the middle of the entrance again. I could hear you from the science section on the second floor."

"That's not fair!" Though I don't really believe it as mortification fills me. I didn't realize I was that loud. I know the library is empty, but that anyone in here just heard my tirade about my awful night and morning makes me want to hide under the desk.

"It is completely fair. I can't have an employee losing their shit in front of others. This situation is bothering you more than you admit. You need to work through it, but not in the workplace. Please take the next three days." He shuts me down immediately, but he's right.

"Fine. I guess I'll leave now then..."

"I'll stop by and check on you later. It's gonna be okay Amb" Nathan hugs me quickly, but I can't make my arms hug him back.

I turn to grab my bag from under the desk. I catch Nathan saying something to Saul out of the corner of my eye. Saul shakes his head and gestures to me before saying something else that seems to have Nathan sagging in relief. I swing the bag over my shoulder. I feel the heat dying down in me.

I'm abandoning Nathan with only Saul. I am mortified. I lost my cool on Saul. He's an idiot, but he didn't need that. I begin my way to the door, still drowning in my mistakes. I feel like my day at least only can go up from here. I grab the wood door's brass handle and swing it open. There's a thunderclap in the distance.

"YOU'VE GOT TO BE FUCKING KIDDING ME!" Fuck it, this day was shit anyway, might as well fucking walk home at this point. I'm already soaked, and it seems like poetic justice. Might as well finish my pathetic sitcom montage of shit. Cue the flashbacks for the last twenty-four hours.

Me showing up happily at the bar for drinks last night.

The night is going downhill when my sister shows up. Cue me laughing with Catherine and Charles as everyone's faces turn from happy to alarmed around me.

Cue the slow-motion slap and Andrew's stupid face in freeze-frames as my palm connects. Then when we took shots at the bar followed by the blackout I don't remember. Nathan's horrified face, as I called my parents. Everything comes to an end as Nathan probably drags mine and

Catherine's lifeless bodies into his apartment.

Fuck everything, I give up.

Chapter Four

I feel a mostly empty tortilla chip bag crunch underneath my head as I roll over. Right now, I don't want to be awake. I reach to check my phone, which is laying a few inches in front of my couch. The T.V. playing Jersey shore reruns. I click the screen twice before picking it up.

"Are you kidding? It's only six-fifty." Why am I up so early? I passed out at three last night. I have too much energy for someone who crashed only four hours ago. Nathan sent me home Saturday morning, and I haven't left my house since. I sit up and sigh. I should really get my shit together. The library is closed on Sunday, so my mandatory three-day break ends tomorrow.

I stand up, and my smell makes me cringe. I need a shower. The room is sad, just like me. Maybe opening some windows will help. I maneuver my way to the windows and open my blinds. Morning sunrise brings a warm glow into my living room. Maybe today things will be okay. A quick shower is all I need to wash myself. I stand and stare at my shampoo for three minutes before groaning and washing my hair really quickly. I only leave the conditioner on long enough to finger detangle my hair before rinsing it out. Meghan, my stylist, would be horrified but what she doesn't know won't hurt her.

My dad called me again last night and against my better judgment, I picked up. I think I was trying to punish myself after getting practically booted from work and sitting alone with my thoughts for way too long. I entertained his ranting as he berated me for being a drunk, and for stirring the pot with my mom. I managed to talk him out of coming home at least and promised to talk to someone about my possible 'problem.' The call ended with him telling me more about the war in the middle east or something. I honestly stopped listening. The call ended with a gruff 'love you' before he hung up.

Getting dressed seems stupid, so I just grab a pair of biker shorts, a sports bra, and t-shirt. I look a bit like a twelve-year-old with my wet hair and a ratty t-shirt but who cares? I walk into my kitchen and look around. My dishes are piled in the sink, I have no clean coffee mugs, and when I open my fridge, I realize I'm out of coffee creamer. "Damnit." I guess I'll go get coffee this morning. I grab my phone and text Catherine, asking if she's busy. But then I realize it's only seven twenty. Surprisingly, I get a text back. She has a doctor's appointment in a few minutes but she can meet me for lunch. I sigh. Guess I'm going solo this morning.

By the front door, I stare at my unicorn satchel and start to unload it. The vibe is off. I pull my little bin of bags out from the shoe rack and start loading my wallet, e-reader, sunglasses, and chapstick into a comically small fuzzy black backpack. Last fall I hot glued googly eyes and fangs to the pocket. It's my fuzzy bat monster and I think it fits the aesthetic of sadness much better. I throw the backpack over my shoulder and step outside, locking the apartment door behind me. The sun is already warm on the pavement even at seven thirty in the morning. I love summer because of the long hours of light and constant warmth, but today it seems annoying. I want to crawl back into my bed and scowl up at the sky as I dig through my bag for oversized sunglasses.

The walk from my apartment to the coffee shop is just a little over ten minutes, but my grumpy attitude means I take almost twenty to wander into the already busy coffee house. The Grove smells like cinnamon, coffee, and the display cases packed with baked goods wafting the fresh bread. There is a line almost to the door, and the massive floor-to-ceiling windows mean the place is cheerfully lit. At least half of the tables lining the windows are full, and another person steps in the door a moment after I do. School is out for the summer, but The Grove and Cici's are constantly busy, kept in business by the locals just as much as the college kids. I don't know how Larry stays in business, his coffee prices almost never go up, and every time he gives me my total I almost feel bad. I'd chalk it up to special treatment for knowing Catherine or something. In reality, I hear his prices are almost as low for everyone else. I can't imagine how he turns a profit.

Last year, Nathan lived above the happy coffee shop, renting the space from the owner, Larry. I was so envious of the space, I can only imagine what it would be like to constantly have a place like this only a few steps away. I'd probably gain thirty pounds. Maybe I should ask if it's still open, though. When Catherine moved out, my ability to pay rent became much harder. It's not that I can't afford it, but I don't know that I want to without someone else living with me.

"Amber?"

I look up into the face of a man, or a boy, I'm not sure. The glasses are vaguely familiar, and the red hair and brown eyes look like... Saul? But that's where the similarities end. This person has a little gold hoop of a nose ring and wavy red hair that sticks up in that artful bedhead way that boys pull off so well. He's got on acid-washed denim jeans and a graphic t-shirt that has a panda-eating pizza. I can see the shape of his lean, muscular body under his clothes. He's got a tan messenger bag slung across his shoulders, and a giant cup of iced matcha tea in his hand. His jeans are cuffed slightly and his Vans look like this is the first time they've ever been out of a box. The only odd thing about the outfit is the orange diving watch. Saul's orange waterproof watch.

"Amber, did you hear me?" The alien alternate-reality version of Saul is staring at me in concern. I am dumbstruck.

I look like a drowned rat. I can feel the damp spot on the back of my shirt, where my wet hair has been lying since I got dressed. I'm pretty sure there is a stain in the middle of this shirt where I dropped hot and sour soup on myself a while ago. There are deep bags under my eyes, I can feel the puffiness of eating only junk food and not sleeping well.

And Saul looks like... That.

"Am I dreaming?" I have to take three big steps because people in front of me have moved and I'm still standing, staring, like an idiot. I turn as I step through, refusing to turn my back on the pretty boy version of Saul standing in front of me. Luckily, he steps with me so I look a small bit less like an idiot.

"What?" He's looking me over like I might be the one who's out of place.

"This is a nightmare, isn't it? I'm dreaming. Hot Saul is a figment of my imagination brought on by junk food and too much reality TV." I pinch the bridge of my nose and close my eyes to focus.

"Hot..." Saul blinks twice and steps closer. He smells amazing. The familiarity of it jars me out of my dazed thoughts. He smells like he did when he hugged me the other day. "What did you just call me?" He looks as put off as I feel.

"What can I get ya, Amber?" I'm next in line. Larry is staring at me with a warm smile that melts the rest of my daze. I can't help but smile back and look at the menu. Larry is always mixing up special drinks in the summer, and this week's special is a honey and vanilla iced latte.

"I'll have a large of the special please." I grin, I need this caffiene.

"Coming right up, my dear." Larry sing-songs his words.

I dig through my wallet for bills, and when Larry sets down a yogurt and fruit parfait with a cake pop I don't even hesitate, "Oh! I love these!"

"That'll be six dollars. You look like you need a good breakfast." Larry winks, and I gather my goods and thank him.

As I turn, I almost run into alien Saul. "Shit, you scared me." I simultaneously attempt to hold all of my things and get the wrapping paper off of the straw. When I almost drop the yogurt, Saul takes the straw and coffee cup from my hands and finishes the job. He doesn't hand it back to me.

"I was going to get one of the outside tables on the patio for a few. Would you like to sit with me?" He holds the door open, still holding my drink. Normally I would tell him, no, but alien Saul has me off my game and I feel myself nodding. He gives me an easy smile, and half of a dimple appears in his right cheek.

Saul sets our cups down at one of the little metal patio tables and pulls the chair out in front of me before motioning for me to sit. Still unsure of what universe I woke up in, I do as directed, and the chair knocks gently into the back of my knees when he scoots it in as I sit, depositing my breakfast on the little rusted table.

"What is happening?" Is the first thing that leaves my mouth as Saul takes the chair next to me.

"Honestly, I was about to ask the same thing. Are you okay?" His red eyebrows draw down slightly in the middle over his wire-framed coke-bottle glasses. They're like the ones Harry Potter wears, but on his face with the nose ring they make him look unassumingly attractive. I want to revolt at my body's reaction to him.

"Am I okay? Who body snatched you?" I sip my latte loudly.

He looks down at himself and back at me like I'm the weird one. "I do own clothes that aren't work clothes, you know?"

"I thought your work clothes were your only clothes." I just wear my normal clothes to work. Are we supposed to have a uniform? Note to self call Nathan about dress code.

He almost has the audacity to look offended. "You thought I wore sweater vests all the time?"

"Saul," I say with as much patience as I can muster, "I'm pretty sure everyone who wears sweater vests, ONLY wears sweater vests."

He laughs. He actually throws his head back and belly laughs. The sound sends tingles dancing up my fingers and into my arms. "Well, I have other clothes."

"And a fucking NOSERING!" I can't let it be any longer.

His face goes pink, and he looks down, still chuckling. "Yeah, that was a mistake in college, but it's been too long now. I couldn't get rid of it. I'd lose my street cred." When he looks back up at me, my heart does some stupid little jump at the amusement twinkling in his eyes. I don't know that he's ever truly looked me in the eye before and it's glorious. I somehow feel like I won.

"Your what?" I've taken exactly one bite from my cake pop. It's five minutes past eight in the morning, and Saul just made a joke about his 'street cred'. I'm pretty sure my dreams couldn't even make up a story this insane.

"Nevermind." He shakes his head, smiling. "So, what has you out this early on a Tuesday?"

"Couldn't sleep." I don't look at him as I mix my yogurt and fruit together. "What are you doing out this early, I thought it was your day off?"

"Oh, it is." He takes a big sip of his iced tea and leans back in his chair. I'm caught off guard by his calm attitude and relaxed posture. His nose ring glints in the morning sunlight and I still don't know how to process the change. "I'm heading into Amish country for the day. Thought I'd do some shopping, have lunch, and hang out for a while."

I snort into my yogurt and side-eye him. "Amish country?"

"Yeah, have you ever been?" He smiles and leans forward in excitement, completely missing the teasing in my voice. "They have tons of little shops full of fun handmade goods. There's this really cute dairy farm that does lunches, and you can tour their facility if you get there early enough. There's also a shop that will let you dip your own candles!"

I'm so thrown off by his excitement, I don't even remember that I should probably make fun of him for this. "I didn't know any of that existed."

"I try to go a few times a year, especially in the spring and summer." Saul smiles again, revealing dimples on both his cheeks.

"Hold up, just a second I need to find my grounding." I take in a big inhale. "So basically you're a boring weirdo librarian by day, and a hot hipster with a nose ring, who goes to Amish country for fun by night?"

"Yes, but I think it's still technically day." He smiles again. Why did no one tell me Saul was hot? "So, what are your plans for today?" I must be staring too much, he's rubbing his neck uncomfortably.

I look away quickly, "Nothing, just headed home to veg on the couch…"

"Well, if you want to reschedule, you can come with me to Amish country." He smiles sweetly.

"What?" I feel like I've been hit by a mac truck and got sent to an alternate reality.

"Sorry, is that weird? I just thought I'd really like to get to know you better. You've had a lot going on and I know for me sometimes getting out helps. I also…" I interrupt him mid-sentence.

"Yes, that sounds great. Like so great, but I can't go like this…" I gesture to my depression chic. "Mind if I run home first?"

"How far do you live? I can drive you and wait in my car." Saul stands up, gathering his things.

"Like a ten-minute walk, I can just walk while you finish." I point in the direction of the apartments.

"Nonsense, grab your food, you can just eat in the car on the way." He grabs my parfait and heads to his car and I follow suit.

What is even happening?

Chapter Five

We go out to the parking lot and he goes to a white vintage truck. It's immaculate, like the ones you see at car shows or in old movies.

"Is this yours?" I stare open-mouthed as Saul looks proud beside me.

"Yep! It's a 1951 Ford F1 pickup. My grandfather left it to me in 2002 when he passed away. I had to completely strip the paint, and it needed a new radiator, the stick shift sucked, so I had to redo the gearshift and timing belt. But I had five years to learn how to drive and it was worth the time. I tried to install seat belts," he looks at me sheepishly, "but it really didn't go super well. There was nowhere to anchor them correctly, and I haven't worried about it. It's only back roads to Amish country though, so if you're worried–"

"You rebuilt the car yourself?" I don't mean to cut him off, but I'm in awe.

"Yeah, I think I was eleven, it was fun to learn. I got books from the library, and my uncle worked in a mechanic shop, so he helped me get the books." He shrugs.

"You learned how to fix a vintage car... when you were eleven... with books?" I can't even put together furniture with the instruction manual.

"Yeah?" He looks confused. "I can read, you know."

"Yeah, that's just super impressive. You didn't have someone to show you?" Who rebuilds a car from scratch solely from books?

"I don't really, 'do people'" Saul air quotes around do people.

I smirk "Does that mean you're a virgin?"

"What?" Saul seems to almost be in a permanent state of confusion.

"You said 'do people'. Like how you say 'do people' for like, sex." God, now I'm the uncomfortable one.

It feels like I can physically see the moment he makes the connection between what he said and the joke I'm making. "Oh, I do people, if you want specifics seventeen people."

"I'm sorry, did you say seventeen?" My brain cannot seem to process the person in front of me.

"Yeah, wait, we are just talking about penetration, right? Because if you want me to add in oral-" He starts using his fingers to count.

"PLEASE STOP!" My face is on fire and I don't think I will ever recover from hearing Saul say penetration. It doesn't even feel like he's bragging just answering ernestly.

"What, you asked?" He tilts his head like a puppy being reprimanded for eating shoes.

"Okay, can we get going before I die then, I'm sorry I asked." I take a dramatic sip of my coffee forcing my mouth shut up.

Saul shrugs and pulls the passenger side door open for me, gesturing with my yogurt that I should get in. As soon as I sit he hands me the parfait and closes the door. My morning of sadness has now turned awkward and I seriously question my mental state. Saul, the sex aficionado with a fancy car who goes to Amish country, has somehow coerced me to go with him. I hop into the ford for an awkwardly quiet drive to the apartments.

I come out of the apartment in a white cotton t-shirt and yellow converse. I thought about putting on a dress, but I don't think I feel quite that great today. I found a nice pair of jean shorts that I think make my butt look great. I can't let 'Hot Saul' show me up all day. I also traded out my sunglasses for a pair of pink heart-shaped ones that Catherine got me for my birthday last year. However, I keep my little black bag to remind me that I still hate the world. I just don't mind the little bubble I'm in at this very moment.

Saul is sitting with the windows down in the truck, and smiles at me as soon as he sees my front door close.

"Ready to go?" He calls when I'm within earshot of him.

"I think so." I open the passenger door and slide in. "How far is the drive, anyway?"

"Probably about twenty minutes on the back roads." He pulls out of the parking lot, and we pass Soups on the way out of town. About four minutes into the drive, I realize it's completely silent.

"Does this thing have a radio?" I have done a really good job of not allowing myself silence the last few days, but the silence of the truck is making my thoughts feel a bit too loud.

"Oh, yeah, it does. I just rarely listen to music." His voice is casual and his eyes don't leave the road.

"Why? I feel like I can't function without music on." I reach for the knobs of the radio.

"I don't know, it just distracts me while I drive." I immediately pull my hand back in fear of him suddenly losing control of the truck if Beyonce comes on.

I stare at him for a while. This man feels like the world's weirdest walking contradiction. I feel drawn to him, but not in a sexy way. In a zoo way. As if I have been delegated to observe a new alien species sent to this planet. A really hot alien, so I guess maybe a little in a sexy way too. But it's Saul.

"Can we talk?" I don't want us to wreck just because I asked him what his favorite color is.

"Yeah, talking is usually fine, but if I take a second to answer, I'm not ignoring you, just processing or getting to a place where I can talk." His eyes are strictly on the road.

"So, what's your favorite thing to do in Amish country?"

"Today I'm hoping the one shop is open to make candles!" He instantly goes from a somber driver to hyper-excited, even though his eyes never leave the road. "So, you can pick your base scent if you want one. It's really cool because it's just some white wax that is already stuck to a string. Or you can choose no scent. I don't normally pick a scent because I can find them overwhelming. Then you walk over to this table that has holes in it. Each hole is a bucket full of different colors of wax. You take your candle by the really long wick and dip it into whatever colors you want. You have to dip it a few times to really get the color to show before moving on to the next one. Then they'll teach you how to make these cool slits in the warm wax while it's still pliable so that you can do rolls and twists to show off all the individual colors. Then they'll cut off the bottom for you and wrap it up. It's one of my favorite things to do."

"You really know a lot about making candles." I say, slightly in awe again at how much he knows.

"It's great too, because they only use beeswax and soy wax, so it's toxin-free and burns super cleanly." He still hasn't looked at me, but he's talked faster and more animatedly. I feel like I'm watching a show. Who needs music when you can watch 'Hot Saul' talk about candles?

"Wait, are regular candles toxic?" I feel a bit of panic. "I have like ten candles in my house. AM I slowly poisoning myself?"

"Short answer yes. Long answer, regular cheap candles are made from paraffin wax, which is a petroleum byproduct. There isn't conclusive evidence, but they think that the black gunk that gathers on the wick is leftover toxic waste from petroleum byproducts. There have been studies done that petroleum byproducts, when burned, can cause problems with respiratory, reproductive, and developmental health. Beeswax is the best wax to burn because it has no naturally occurring toxins. It actually has been proven to be a natural air purifier. Beeswax is also great because it's stable on its own. People that are vegan don't like to use beeswax, even though it's important to do things like clear out bee hives to help them produce and colonize better. But anyway, soy is technically safe, but it's not stable alone, so most of the time to make vegan candles they'll still use paraffin to help stabilize the candle. Soy also burns really quickly. The Amish believe in all-natural, so they only use beeswax." He stops talking abruptly and looks at me out of the corner of his eye. It's the only time I've seen his eyes leave the road.

"Sorry, was that too much?" His face flushes.

"You are so smart." I am in awe of the man next to me.

"I'm not smart, I just remember a whole bunch of stupid useless stuff. It's a curse really, I cannot find a beeswax candle that smells like birthday cake, and that used to be my favorite scent" He sighs.

"You literally just SAVED MY LIFE!" I laugh.

"There is no conclusive proof…" He starts to stutter out.

"But there is more proof that it's bad than good. I think it's super cool you know so much. You're practically google." I flash a big first grade smile at him.

He laughs and turns down a different road flanked on both sides by corn. "We're almost there, now."

"I have never been so excited to make candles in my life." I could jump up and down. But I won't, that'd be weird.

Saul turns and looks at me, smiling like a little kid. The half dimple on his right cheek shows, making him look even younger. Little butterflies jump around in my stomach and I'm surprised by the way I feel. 'Hot Saul' is really scrambling my brain. We ride for the last five minutes in comfortable silence and I enjoy the sun through the windows. A cute little town comes into view, with pretty wooden houses, massive trees, and people sprinkled all over the open town square. Most of the women are in long neutral-colored dresses and white bonnets, and the men are in their neutral-colored shirts and pants with black suspenders and black hats. There is a small parking lot behind a massive white barn that reminds me of a plane terminal, and there is some street parking that seems to be mostly filled by horses and open-top buggies.

Saul glances at his watch and then over at me as we pull into a parking spot by the giant metal building. "The dairy tour starts at nine-thirty. We are just in time. Is that something you'd want to do?"

"Well, I have never seen a dairy farm before, so that sounds great!" I think these yellow converse are working. "Can I feed a baby cow?"

"A calf? Yeah probably." Saul pulls up to a massive barn. I couldn't tell in the distance, but the barn was like out of a movie with a serene pasture behind it filled with cows. As we pull in closer, I take in how large the barn is. It's almost as big as the library.

"Here we are." Saul parks the truck outside the barn door in a patch of gravel. I turn to look at him, but his door already shuts and he's walking in front of the truck.

Well, alright then I guess we're going. I turn to open the door and put my hand on the handles and there Saul is; already swinging it open for me. He smiles and lifts his hand for me to use to get down. I reach for his hand and use it for support to get out. It's rough and callused, he doesn't seem like a hard labor guy. But in truth he is nothing like I thought he seemed like in the first place.

I smile at him, his eyes a lovely deep brown. He has beautiful long lashes and...

"Excuse me?"

I drop Saul's hand, realizing I held it as we were staring, smiling at each other. We both blush and turn to the man speaking to us. He looks a lot like Larry but with a beard, Amish garb and both arms. What if it's Larry in disguise? No, this guy has two real arms and Larry doesn't bother with a prosthetic anyway.

"We're here for the dairy tour, Zakariah." Saul says cordially. Does he really come so much he knows peoples names?

"Oh, I'm sorry Saul, the tour already started and it's a school group so I can't put you in with them." Zakariah is very apologetic.

"So I can't feed a baby cow?" I look up at Saul disappointed.

"Well, if you just wanna feed a calf, I was just going to feed the new calf, Ruth. I have no problem passing off chores." Zakariah smiles kindly, he has kind eyes like Larry. He waves us to follow him into the barn.

"CAN WE!" I look to Saul for permission.

"Of course, if that's what you want." Saul starts to smile, but I don't wait for it and run after the Amish man.

"ZAKARIAH WAIT UP!" I go chasing after him, leaving Saul in the dust. I'm pretty sure I can hear Saul's laughter behind me, but I'm too distracted by the barn doors opening. I catch a whiff of manure and hay that slows my pace slightly. But even gross animal smells can't keep me away from the brown-eyed, knobby-kneed calf that Zakariah is leading my way. He is holding a massive bottle in one hand he offers to me when I'm close enough. It has the biggest baby bottle top I've ever seen. It reminds me of the finger of a surgical glove.

"Just hold it up in front of her face like this," Zakariah helps me hold it so that the sweet calf can drink from it. "Let me know if you get tired."

"I don't think I will." I smile up at him. "You know, you remind me of someone."

"You know, I hear that a lot. My sister's son lives in Bethton Grove, and anyone who visits from there says we look just alike."

"Oh," I laugh. "You do. Does that mean Larry is Amish?"

"I mean, no," Zakariah says. "He left when he was eighteen. Felt the Lord called him to other places. But he is always welcome here. He still has Christmas with us every year, and is always around if a barn needs raising."

"Well, I can't argue." I say as Saul comes into my line of sight. "Larry is a cornerstone of Bethton Grove. I think we'd crumble without him." Then something occurs to me. "How did Larry lose his arm?"

Ruth finishes her bottle and nuzzles at my hands. When I look back at Zakariah, he's smiling, looking between Saul and me. I realize he still hasn't answered my question.

"My nephew is a truly extraordinary man." He takes Ruth's lead and directs her back toward the pen she was in before.

Saul gives me a puzzled look, and I shrug. "Why did you ask about Larry's arm?"

"Have you never wondered how he lost it?" I shrug.

"I guess I haven't. I didn't know that I was supposed to." Saul taps his chin, and furrows his brow.

I laugh, and Saul calls goodbye to Zakariah as we head out of the barn. It's getting really warm outside as we walk toward the dirt path that seems to trail into town. We pass the cow pasture, and horse barn on the way. I can hear a chicken coop in the distance.

"It's been a running joke for years. I'm pretty sure no one knows how he lost his arm. The first time I asked him, he told me about a shark attack. If you ask Catherine, though, her aunt claims the military took it to clone him." I ponder on the grand mystery that is Larry.

"That all seems a bit ridiculous." Saul says skeptically.

"I think that's the point by now. The more ridiculous it is, the more it seems plausible."

He looks puzzled, but doesn't say anything else as we come into the town square. There is a cute little park in the middle full of beautiful flowers, and a few Amish children in dresses play with chalk. It's getting increasingly warmer, and I feel exponentially lighter since leaving my apartment this morning. I chance a look at Saul, who's tapping his fingers on his chest as we walk. It sort of looks like he's playing piano, and I wonder what he's thinking about. His face is peaceful and I still can't seem to get over the complete contradiction he is when he's not working.

"So, where is the candle shop?" I ask when we come to a crossroads.

"It's the building with the blue door. Is that where you want to go next?" He's still drumming his fingers on his chest. I want to ask him about it, but he doesn't even seem to notice he's doing it.

"I thought that's why we are here." I smile at him because he seems unsure of himself suddenly. "You made it sound so great in the car. I am really excited!"

"Okay, then let's go in." Saul says.

Chapter Six

The bell chimes as we push inside of the little candle shop. The place is cool, thankfully. Floor to ceiling shelves line three of four walls of the shop. They're organized by colors, scents, and size. It's mesmerizing, and I have to stare for a few minutes to feel like I absorb it all.

"Good morning!" A cheery young woman walks out from the back room. She has on a pale pink dress and a white apron. Her white bonnet covers her hair and the little straps hang down on either side of her face. "Hi Saul! I was hoping you'd be back in soon! It's late for you to show up, I didn't think you were coming today. I just got some new mica powders in, I thought of you when I mixed up the glittery orange."

Saul smiles widely at the woman. "Good morning, Martha! I'm excited to see it." He turns his attention momentarily to me, and touches my elbow for half a second before moving his hand and taking a step toward Martha. My skin tingles from the barely there contact, and I look between the two people who seem to be such good friends. "This is my fr–" he pauses for half a second and then clears his throat. "This is Amber."

A twinge of guilt courses through me. I'm truly an asshole. I have been an asshole for so long that Saul couldn't, or didn't want to introduce me as a friend. I guess until now, we haven't been.

Martha gives me a smile and steps forward, offering her hand. "It's nice to meet you, Martha. Saul has been talking all morning about how great this place is!" I smile back at him, but he's looking at a little display table with candles on it, tapping his fingers again.

"Well, you two can come on back with me, I'll get you started. "How many are you planning to make today, Saul? Two like usual?"

He nods distractedly. "Please, and one for Amber." He's studying an intricately carved candle full of every color of the rainbow. It reminds me of those twisted rainbow suckers that we used to get at the fair as kids.

When Martha motions us back, Saul brushes his fingers against my arm again and we walk back together. Martha grabs our wicks and explains picking scents to me before the bell above the door out in the gift shop chimes again.

"I'll get that. I'm sure that Saul can help you with the rest. He knows where everything is." She smiles at me again. I understand why he likes it here. It's great. It smells floral and warm. I pick up a few of the scented wicks, deciding between orange blossom, lemon lavender, and one called pine forest. I decide on the lemon lavender and wander over to where Saul is standing patiently watching me.

The back room has the same floor to ceiling shelves, but instead of the fourth wall being a register, there is a giant work bench set up. When I step closer to look, the L-shaped wooden table has holes cut into the top where basins rest filled with different colors of melted wax.

"How do I start?"

"Come over here and I'll show you." Saul demonstrates once. He holds the starter wick under for three seconds and then pulls it back out to let it drip for maybe ten seconds before repeating the process. He then shows me where the cool water is and explains to dip the candle in the cool water between colors. Just for a second to make sure you mix nothing. The process is slow and tedious and it makes sense that Saul likes it. While I struggle to be still, Saul seems to enjoy the slow methodical movements.

He hands the candle back to me and I dip it a few more times in the lavender color he did first, waiting until I can't see any of the starter wick under. It's silent in the back room. I've heard the bell over the door jingle twice since Martha left, so it's safe to say that for now we are alone. I think it's interesting that Saul knows Martha personally. I wonder how often he's out here. She already knew how many candles he wanted and everything.

"Do you come out here and make candles a lot?" My voice seems to echo around the quiet room. I almost feel embarrassed about how little I know of Saul. He may be annoying at work, but he's been at the Library for almost a year and I have done everything in my power to stay away from him.

"I like to come twice a month, but that isn't always possible." He mumbles, focused on the drip of a robin's egg blue that is rolling down his candle.

I nod and dip my candle in the water before switching to a bright sunshine yellow. "What do they use to dye the wax?" I ask when it feels too quiet again.

Saul seems distracted, but he pushes his glasses up his nose and looks my way. "That depends. Commercial candles are just synthetic dyes. Think, whatever stuff they use to make crayons. The best colors are things that naturally occur in nature. Paprika, Turmeric, Clove, Saffron, Lavender. Those materials also burn rather cleanly and emit small amounts of smell. But mica powder is also common because it mixes well with synthetic wax like paraffin and also things like soy and beeswax. Though, if the ratios are off it can clog the wick. It's why colors are so light and you have to dip them a few times to get a true color. You can't use too much. It looks really pretty in wax melts though. That's what makes them sparkle. Most of these pigments are made from herbs, spices, and things naturally occurring in nature though. Just some of the colors–like the orange–are mica." Saul clears his throat after the last words, and I can tell he seems uncomfortable.

"Is something wrong?" I ask hesitantly, trying to decide if I've somehow made him uncomfortable with my questions.

He clears his throat again and gives me a really weird smile that looks more like he might throw up. "No, not at all. I'm sorry if I'm talking too much. Sometimes I get caught up on things..." He trails off and looks back to his candles. One is now taking on a beautiful blue marbled effect, and I wonder how he's done it.

I switch to a bright green color. "No, I don't think you're talking too much. I like it."

He laughs uncomfortably. "You can tell me when I'm talking too much. You won't hurt my feelings. I know I ramble sometimes."

"No, really." I stop what I'm doing and turn to him. "I like it, I like hearing about all of the stuff you know. I'm sorry I never really listened before. You're like, really smart. And really interesting. I'm having a really good time today, and if I'm asking questions, I want to know the answer."

Saul looks like he'd like to melt into candle wax right then. He nods, though, and turns back to what he's doing.

"So, what color do each of the different additives make the wax?" I ask to try and get him to talk.

"Saul looks at me for a long moment before answering. "Well, turmeric is a bright yellow, like mustard color. Saffron is an orange red mix depending on how much you use. But since saffron is a ridiculously expensive substance, it wasn't used except in really expensive candles. Multiple colors of rose make lots of different reds and pinks. So usually they were gathered and dried before being crushed into powder to mix in. Rosemary is one of my favorite colors." He pauses, looking at the basins of wax. "It's close to this color." He points to an almost ashy olive green. It's a bit of an odd color if I'm being honest, it reminds me of the toads that we used to find in the garden as kids.

"So, how do they add the colors? I can't imagine that water mixes well with beeswax."

Saul does this sort of huff through his nose, and an amused look glitters in his eyes. The ghost of his half dimple shows as well and I find myself staring at it, staring at him. "No, you can't mix water." He holds up his one finished candle. "Most of the time they'd extract pigment from whatever they were using. Sometimes, if it was flowers or something, they'd dry it and then grind it into a paste that they'd mix into melted wax. Other times pigment can be extracted using acids and bases. Like if you steep flowers like marigolds in water and wait for the water to turn yellow, you can then mix something like baking soda in to make a bright yellow pigment. But if you mix in an acid, the color turns more of a burnt orange. That takes a long time, though, and the colors are photosensitive. So if they're in the sun, they'll fade."

By now, I've forgotten my candle. I'm so fascinated by the man standing in front of me. I feel like I've woken from a daze. It's like I'm seeing the world with Saul in it for the first time. I can't believe I haven't been able to truly see it until now.

"Do you want me to show you how to carve flowers into your candle?" Saul is staring back at me, he seems to have forgotten his other candle and is reaching for mine.

"I would love that!"I smile ear to ear.

"I'm so sorry for the delay! I guess today is going to be a busy day! How are things going, Saul?" Martha walks back into the back room, smiling at us. She walks over to one of the shelves, and grabs a few wrapped candle sets.

"Great, I found the orange you were talking about. You're right Martha, it's lovely."

"Why did the orange make you think of Saul?" I ask.

Martha laughs a bit and walks back out to the showroom. "He's had that orange watch for as long as I've known him. Every time I see a bright orange, I can only think of Saul."

I look at the watch and smile. Saul doesn't seem to really notice. He's grabbing a tool that reminds me of a potato peeler and shows me for the next ten minutes how to put pretty little flowers into my candle. By the time he's done, you can see all the layers of colors I've put into the candles. I love it.

Saul's watch beeps as we are walking up to the front of the store to pay. He looks down at it and frowns. "I'm gonna have to head back." He says, quickly.

"Okay? We haven't been here very long, is everything okay?"

"Yeah," He says distractedly, paying for his candles and mine before I have a chance to pull my wallet out. "I just have to put my laundry in the dryer."

"Uh, what?" Is he trying to ditch me on whatever this thing we're doing is.

"My laundry. If I don't do it on the second alarm, I'll forget it in the washing machine for like six days and it will stink and I'll have to wash it again."

"Why don't you just change your alarm." Am I losing it? Is this a fever dream?

"I can't. That doesn't work. I always do my laundry on Tuesdays. I put the clothes in the washing machine while my coffee pot runs in the morning and I have to change it over by two. Any later and I won't have the energy to fold it and put it away. But if I change my alarm, I'll forget. And I really hate the smell of my laundry when it sits. I hate the smell of bleach even more. And bleach is the only way to get rid of stale laundry scent." There is not a hint of sarcasm or amusement on his face.

"Oh, okay..." Is this a joke? I follow behind him as he walks out of the building. Is this pay back for all the times I treated him like dirt? We walk up to the white truck and he opens my door and helps me in. I really screwed up, I was so judgemental of him. Saul starts up the ford, and it purrs to life. I shouldn't judge a book by its cover. He backs out of his parking spot. Wait, if he just brought me out here to ditch me on a date as payback, then he's the jerk. Saul heads back on the country roads to Bethton Grove. So I was right about him. Wait, is this even a date, I just tagged along, but it feels like a date.

"Did I do something?" It's better to just get on with this.

Saul looks away from the road abruptly, studying my face for what feels like a small eternity. "I don't think so? What do you mean?"

"Are you kidding? Who ditches someone for laundry?" I feel heat rise up in me.

"You can come back to my house and do laundry with me if you want..." His voice trails off.

WHAT IS HAPPENING? I take in a deep breath. "What is happening right now?"

"I was about to ask you the same thing. Did I do something wrong? I didn't intend to make you feel left out. I can tell you're mad at me now. I didn't think it was that big of a deal. I'm not ditching you. I just have things I have to do today. If you want to come with me, you can. I am having a really good day with you. I'm sorry if laundry ruins it." He is starting to look genuinely panicked, drumming his fingers on the steering wheel hard. The world passes by us in a blur as I turn in the seat to look at him.

"Are you actually being serious? I've been so mean to you?" I am confused but glad he doesn't hate me. Oh, which still makes me the bad guy.

"I don't think you're mean. When have you been mean to me? I mean, I know you were a little upset the other morning. But that's okay, we all have off days. I know sometimes I want to scream, too." There is the smallest bit of relaxation in his features now. His fingers are still tapping away though, which seems to tap into my brain, scrambling my thoughts.

"I constantly am yelling at you over breaking the computers, and you don't hate me for that?" Am I bad at being mean? I was trying to be mean then.

"Oh, that. I mean, I just appreciate how much you help me. I feel terrible when I do things wrong. I just really struggle with technology sometimes." His eyes don't leave the road but I can see him chewing on his cheek.

"We both know this isn't a normal conversation, right?" He is clueless.

He pauses, staring really hard out the front window. HIs knuckles are white against the steering wheel. "I really want to say yes… But now I'm just as lost as you are." He sighs deeply. "I don't normally like to say anything, but at this point, I feel a bit like you might jump out of my car at any moment." He takes another deep steadying breath and I find myself leaning closer, suddenly concerned for what he's about to tell me.

"I'm considering it." I attempt the joke but his eyes leave the road in a panic for half a second as he looks at me like he's assessing if he's going to have to grab me or something.

"I have Autism. I don't normally tell people because they get super weird about it. But I'm very obviously missing important things in our communication, and I don't know what it is. I'm sorry. So if you wouldn't mind, can we just back up like five minutes and start over? Can you tell me where I went wrong, confused you, or explained myself poorly?" His voice shakes.

Confusion and relief and utter horror courses through me as I look back on every single interaction Saul and I have had in the last year. I kind of want to puke because I am definitely the biggest asshole there could possibly be.

"Amber?" His voice quivers.

"Yeah, we can. At least we're both confused now? I think one piece was 'I assumed you secretly hated me'." I sigh.

"What? I think you're amazing." I can only see his profile, but his ears are bright pink and that dimple . "You're one of the coolest people I have met in a long time. I love your style, and you're always so interesting and you are so funny."

"I guess until today I couldn't say the same about you. I really, really hate being called in on my off days." I twiddle my thumbs ashamedly.

"I'm sorry. I don't mean to call you so much. You're just so much easier to talk to than Nathan. He doesn't walk me through how to do it. He just does it. Honestly, I just don't want him thinking I can't handle things. I look up to him and he is extremely intimidating sometimes."

"He is an actual teddy bear, and about as smart sometimes." I laugh. "I guess I didn't see it that way. I'm just doing something or have plans. It really sucks to have to change... your plans... Like how you didn't want to change yours. Ooooooh." Well now I really am the bad guy.

"You haven't seen Nathan blow his top before have you... Oh, wait, you're talking about the laundry." He winces. "I get that. I guess I should have explained myself better. And I'll do better about not calling you as much." He smiles sheepishly at me. "I really have had fun with you today." There's three minutes of silence, and I start to recognize that we are getting closer to Bethton Grove. Saul's alarm goes off again, and he silences it quickly. "If you promise to remind me about laundry when we get back into town, do you want to stop somewhere and have lunch with me?"

"Well, I don't have plans for the day and I have to make up for assuming you hate me. Let's go do your laundry first. I'd be frustrated if my plans changed too." I feel weird, but a happy weird.

Chapter Seven

Saul ran into his house while I sat in his truck. I still couldn't believe that he owned the place. I have been living in an apartment my entire adult life since I left college. I can't imagine what it would be like to own a house. Saul was pretty singularly minded, so I didn't have a chance to ask him about it. Within ten minutes, he's running back out his front door, turning to lock it and bolting for the truck.

With a smile, he opens his driver's side door. I've turned on the bench seat to lean against the passenger door and pull my legs up. As he slides in, an alarm on his phone goes off again. He turns it off without even looking at it and puts the key in the old ignition of the car.

"What was that one for?"

"Oh, that was just the second, reminding me of laundry, but I just did it." We back out of his driveway. "So, lunch?"

Fifteen minutes later, we pull into a McDonald's parking lot. There isn't technically one in town. Just like there aren't any other major chains or grocery stores. So we have to cross the freeway to find the first one. It's next to a gas station and across the street from a massive dollar store. There isn't much else around this freeway exit. There is a small drive-thru line, but it looks like there is all of one family with too many kids, and an old couple sitting inside.

We walk side by side and order at one of those little contactless kiosks. I normally just go up to the counter at a place like this, but Saul kind of insisted. He also insisted on paying for lunch as well, since he had been rude earlier. I argued, but it was pointless. Part of me was grateful. The library salary kept me alive, housed, fed, and I always had some money set aside to do things, but it's not like I'm rolling in cash.

Saul and I walk away from the kiosk. "So where should we sit?"

"I always sit by the big window next to the street." Saul says, nodding to the back corner. "But wherever you want sounds fine."

"If there's a slug-bug, can I punch you?" I say with a smirk.

"Uh, I guess?" He looks at me, confused.

"Cool, let's sit." I lead the way to the table and Saul follows closely behind. There's a small white table right in front of the window next to the street. I slide into the metal chair on one side and he slides into the other across from me. He looks out the window for a moment and my eyes follow his. This is a nice view, watching all the cars drive past. Passed the small road behind the McDonalds is an abandoned old barn and farmhouse surrounded by an overgrown field. The windows in the house are boarded up but you can tell this house was a stunning old brick farmhouse when it was in its prime.

"You see that house? I'd love to buy it, restore it and turn it into a B&B." Saul points out the window.

"Oh, really?" I turn and look at Saul. His eyes shimmer a little in the light like amber glass. A gentle smile spreads across his face. He's off in his own world when the McDonald's worker drops food at our table. We both say our 'thank yous' and pull our food from the tray. I grab my 10-piece nugget with fries and a coke. While Saul slides himself his big mac, large fry, and sprite. I can't wait and pop a fry into my mouth.

"Oh my god, how are McDonald's fries so good?" I grab another to cram into my mouth. "French fries are my kryptonite."

"Did you know McDonald's actually changed their fry recipe in the early nineteen nineties?" He says after he takes a drink of sprite.

"I didn't." I open the Ranch sauce that goes with my nuggets.

"Yeah, from the forties to the nineties they used beef tallow to fry the french fries. They called it 'recipe forty-seven' and it supposedly made... You're looking at me weird." Saul stumbles over his words.

"No, I'm not?" Honestly, I am though. I could listen to him talk all day. I kick myself for the hundredth time today for not listening to him sooner.

"Yes, you are?" Saul deflates a little and I rush to explain myself, hoping I haven't somehow done something wrong..

"I guess I am. I just really like to listen to you. It's like a podcast." His voice is soothing.

"Uh, I'm not really sure how I'm supposed to feel about that. Are you just using me for your personal entertainment?" He's giving me a weird look now.

"No, well, kind of. I just love to learn stuff. Your voice is super soothing and I just like that you want to tell me all of this. You found something cool and you wanna share it with me. It makes me feel kind of… special." I feel my cheeks flush as I watch him turn bright pink.

It feels weird to admit how much today has changed my opinion of him. It also feels weird to share this level of honesty with someone. I enjoy honesty, but after talking in the car earlier I feel the strain of saying exactly what I'm thinking so that there is no confusion. I should have realized sooner that half truths were part of the problem. Saul takes everything at face value, even if there is a secondary meaning in what I say.

"Oh well, uh, thanks." He rubs his neck uncomfortably.

"Tell me more!" I ask to hopefully make him less uncomfortable.

"I kind of lost my train of thought." Saul stammers.

"That's okay, I remember you were telling me about 'recipe forty-seven'." I smile widely at him.

"Oh, you were actually listening? I really appreciate it, not a lot of people do." Saul laughs, but I can hear a hurt behind it.

"Really? They are missing out then." I say, stuffing another chicken nugget, soaked in ranch, into my mouth. I am pretty sure he's blushing, because he looks down at his food for a long time before he says anything.

"Well, I was going to say that sometime around the nineties–some dude I think named Phil–had a heart attack. He blamed companies for using saturated fats in their foods. He paid someone to change billboards in time square to villainize restaurants. Eventually, he targeted McDonald's specifically. They changed their oil to a mix of canola and soy oil, and people boycotted their fries for a while. The solution they came up with was to fry their fries before freezing and shipping them. The only way they've managed to keep their fries crispy is by doing this. Although in the mid-two-thousands there was a group of people who did some blind taste tests as well as actual health comparisons between the two methods for making fries and tallow wins out every single time. But, now the world has made anything like that 'the enemy' so they'll never be able to go back to their old ways." Saul makes air quotes with his fingers when he says the enemy.

I take another bite of the fry in my hand and stare at it intently. I have a feeling if I stay around this boy much longer, my entire perception of the world will shift. Who knew the sweater vests hid so much? "Honestly, that's amazing. How do you learn all these things?"

Saul shrugs. "Usually, I'll see something on the TV or someone I know will say something and it will spark my interest. Then, once I know something, it just gets filed away in my brain and sometimes I'll forget until someone else says something. Then it just pops out of my mouth before I even realize what's happening. I don't really have a ton of control over it. My favorite show as a kid was that one that's called 'How It's Made.'"

"Oh, I loved that show too! My sister thought it was weird..." I trail off.

"So, do you want to talk more about whatever happened with your sister?" Saul is looking at the window and not at me.

My insides go cold and now it's my turn to look anywhere but at him. With the weird whirlwind that today had turned into, I momentarily forgot my misery. "I don't know. We just had this massive falling out a few years ago. It caused a ton of family stress, and we just haven't talked since." I sigh, chancing a look at him.

Saul has his hands in his lap, staring at me intensely. There's a look of concern and understanding etched across his face. He opened his mouth like he might ask a question, but then he closed it again. I realized he was waiting for me to say more.

My phone vibrates annoyingly on the table and we both glance at it. It's a succession of three text messages from an unknown number.

Unknown: I know things haven't gotten off on the right foot, but we really should talk.

Unknown: This is Andrew. I know you probably are just going to delete this, but please consider it. You didn't even give us a chance to explain.

Unknown: Let's meet at Cici's at seven if you want. Or if you want to meet somewhere else I'm flexible.

I lay my head on the table and groan.

"What?" Saul cocks his head to the side.

"We spoke of the devil and now he's texting me..." I sit up and toss my head back and groan again. "And he wants to meet up."

"This is your sister's husband, right? Do you want to meet up with him?" Saul takes a big bite of his big mac.

"Yes, and no." I sigh, "He is the Devil incarnate but..."

"But what? I don't really understand why you're conflicted. If he's that bad, stay away." He doesn't sound sure of himself as he says it, though.

"I miss having a family. I'm conflicted because what if things get better, but also what if it doesn't and I've put myself through it all for nothing." I start peeling at the side of my nails. "I just don't know how to handle it all. They showed up out of nowhere after YEARS and want to fix things with no warning."

"I mean, maybe things have changed? I can't speak to whether or not it's worth it though. I personally think most things are worth it, even if the outcome is wrong. But I don't ever want to be the kind of person who gives up without exhausting all of my options. Even if that means I get hurt a little. I'd rather end up a little hurt than always looking back wondering if I did something wrong." Saul says matter-of -factly before he takes a huge bite of his big mac.

"My heart wants to agree but my brain is still on the fence. I might as well, right? I can only punch Andrew so many times before he leaves me alone." I sigh.

"Punch?" He looks confused and alarmed, but continues on his train of thought anyway. "I can understand being conflicted. Putting yourself out there is scary. No one likes to feel out of control. I always struggle in important situations with people because I rarely feel like I'm in control. There is always the disconnect between my personal understanding of a situation and what someone is saying, and what they actually mean. Usually I find parts of the situation that I can control that make me feel like I have more power. Like picking the time and place where I can talk. And giving myself an escape route if I need one. I also try to control situations by initiating the questions so that I can start a conversation to set myself up to understand and be understood."

"Oh, I can do that. If I completely control the situation, nothing can go wrong!" I pull out my phone and text Andrew back.

Me: Cici's at 7 I can leave when I want and if you touch me again, you will get hurt.

"Uhh..." Saul leans forward over the table a bit. "That's not what I meant."

"Well, that's what I heard. I feel so much better, You are such a confidence booster, Saul." I smile bright at him. He laughs, shakes his head, and takes another bite.

Chapter Eight

"If you need me later, I'll be around. I just have some family things to do this afternoon. But text me an SOS if things get bad. I can call you and pretend to be a dying aunt or something." Saul is leaning against the driver's door.

"My dying aunt probably isn't a good idea since Andrew is related to me." I grimace at my own words. I hate saying that.

Saul shrugs. "That's what my female friends in college always used to ask me to do. I still don't get why they didn't just leave." He opens the door to his truck.

"Men are scary, they don't often accept people leaving mid dinner. Especially men like Andrew." I think of him grabbing me after he cheated with Brittany and shutter. Honestly, I'm feeling less confident now that some time has passed since I sent the text. The fallout from the other night still feels too close and I'm not sure that I trust Andrew to handle things the right way. He's always been a little manipulative, but the anger in his expression the other night felt different than it did years ago when we dated.

"I mean, I know it's rude to just leave, but if you're not vibing... why suffer through an entire interaction." He sits in his car. "I know it's probably just me."

"It definitely is. One time like two years ago I tried online dating and this guy thought we had such great chemistry, he somehow managed to get me to go back to his house, and I had to pretend I started my period and hid in the bathroom for like 45 minutes because I didn't know what to do. He even said it didn't bother him and he was 'willing to bone either way'. I had to fake unbearable cramps and texted Nathan to come get me. Then the guy texted me so many times I eventually lied and said I moved to Georgia. He was so mad at me he sent me awful texts for days until I blocked his number. Even though he lived forty minutes away I was afraid to leave the house for like a month because I was worried he'd come looking for me." I cringe after realizing I just told him that story. No one but Catherine and Nathan knew it. Saul just has a way to pull all information out of me, without even trying. "But thank you for offering to bail me out. Hopefully, I don't need it." There's a small nagging feeling in the back of my mind that I keep pushing down. I can stay in control and be fine.

I wave as he pulls away, and he gives me a smile that has a hint of a dimple showing in his cheeks.

Inside my apartment things feel empty and quiet. There's an annoying amount of dishes in the sink that I don't feel like dealing with right now, and trash sitting on the coffee table that I know I should pick up. But my lack of sleep is catching up, and I still have four hours until dinner. I decide bed and a nap is the way to go if I plan to be even remotely ready for the conversation with Andrew tonight.

I sigh as I pick up snacks laying on my bed from last night and put them on my night table. I just don't have the energy. I collapse into my bed, pull the covers over my head, check that my phone alarm is set for six and close my eyes.

One of the stupid preset alarm tones chimes through my mind, shattering the warmth I'd drifted into. I groan and for a second consider texting Andrew that I'm not coming and going back to bed. I can't though, if I don't get this over with, they'll just keep trying. Better now than later I tell myself.

I get up and head to the bathroom. In the mirror I still look tired, but not as bad as I did this morning. I forgo any makeup, I'm not trying to impress anyone. Aside from changing my shirt to something with sleeves for the chill of the bar. I'm ready to go. I decide to leave so that I can get there first and find a table.

The bar is pretty dead compared to most nights. A group of men including Andrew's dad sit at the bar watching a sports channel on the TV. I wonder for a second how Mr. Brinks feels about Andrew being home. I wonder if he knows everything that happened between us. He has his back to me, a few empty bottles already lined up in front of him. I wonder what he'd think if he saw Andrew and I sitting here together tonight over drinks. Does he even know that his son is sitting less than thirty feet away from him?

I sit at the table in the middle of the room facing the door. If I am in control of everything, it will all be. I'll see Andrew coming in. I can make an escape to the door anytime. I look at my phone, my list of questions sit on my notes app. I know everyone here.

Larry walks to the table, "Hey sweetie, want your usual lemon drop?"

"Not tonight, I'm waiting on Andrew, I think it's best if I just have soda water and lime." I smile uncomfortably.

"Andrew, huh?" Larry looks at me skeptically. "Do we need to set up a boxing ring?"

I laugh uncomfortably as the anxiety flares in my stomach. "I promise to be on my best behavior tonight. That's part of why I'm going with non-alcoholic."

Larry smiles and nods before turning away. "Just give me a heads up this time if you're going to swing," He calls over his shoulder. "I want to get it on camera!"

I sit quietly tapping my fingers on the old fake wood table. Marked with names and scratches telling the story of its life. I feel both anxiety and anger. My heart feels as if it could burst from my chest. That'd be a sight, hey Andrew how are you, oh that, that's my heart you destroyed, why, don't you stomp on it while you're here.

"Here you go sweetie." Larry sets down a glass of soda water with lemon wedge on the side and walks off.

I mumble to myself "I asked for lime." One thing wrong isn't bad and it's just water. Take a deep breath and…

Andrew is ten minutes late. It's fine I keep telling myself, it will be fine. It doesn't mean anything. Two things being off aren't a big deal. It's just lemon, and ten minutes could be traffic... in Bethton Grove... on a Tuesday.

"Hey Amber." A voice behind me says, causing me to jump. WHY IS HE BEHIND ME?

"Uh, hey Andrew, I didn't see you come in." Play it cool Amber. Deep breath, you are still in control of yourself and the situation.

"Oh, I parked behind, so I just came in the back door." Andrew slides into the chair across from me.

I feel off my game already, nothing is quite right. I stare at Andrew from across the table and take a long drink of my soda water. Andrew makes eye contact with Larry over my shoulder and flags him down. Neither of us have directly spoken to each other and while he talks to Larry, I study him. I feel like I didn't get a good look at him a few days ago.

In essence he still seems the same, but somehow he looks like a different person. His face is a different shape, and stubble covers his less angular jaw. He's gained weight. It strikes me as funny because he always cared so much about his looks. There's something else off about him that I can't quite place, some sort of chaotic furious energy that gives me goosebumps. Was he always like this and I didn't notice? I place my phone on the table tapping the screen to check the time.

IT'S AT 1%?

How did it get that low? Because you've been out all day and haven't had a freaking charger. I can maintain control, I'll just not mess with it until I have to.

"Uh... So are you still working at the Library?" Andrew asks.

I refrain from rolling my eyes. "I feel like you should just start this conversation since you're the one who wants to be here. If you're going to waste my time, I will be leaving."

"Always so honest, you haven't changed at all." There's ice in his tone and goosebumps rise on my skin. I feel like I'm staring at a stranger.

I clench my fists under the table, I can't tell if he meant to be insulting, but it sure felt like it. I want to shout across the table that he's wrong. Because I have chosen to change every part of myself to be nothing like the person he knew. I keep my mouth shut, though, deter-mined to make him do all the talking. I'll prove to him I've changed by refusing to react to the bait he's so obviously holding in front of me.

"You have, I see." I slowly look him up and down with a smirk.

"I have, more than you realize. Just like Brittany has. You need to give us a chance. Brittany loves you. She has always idolized you as her big sister." He smiles smugly and places his hand on my hand that's next to my phone. "We love you, we are here to be a family." The lie rolls from his mouth way too easily, but his eyes glitter at me like we're sharing some secret.

"Do you not remember what happens when you touch me? Or do you need a reminder?" I slide my hand out from under his.

"You mean assault? That I continue to kindly not press charges on you about." He raises an eyebrow.

"You touched me every time first I could charge you for the same." I stare through him already plotting my escape.

He takes a deep breath and sighs. I can see him grit his teeth. "The past is in the past. We're past that and now we can reconcile and work through this childish mess."

"Reconciling requires forgiveness and you haven't even asked for that." I cross my arms, I can feel rage boiling inside me.

"Isn't us being here asking for a relationship good enough? How is that not asking for forgiveness?" I can feel the vibration of the table as his leg bounces up and down. His tone is becoming more clipped with every exchange we have like he's already tired of talking to me. Feeling's mutual buddy.

"See you have to apologize first to ask for forgiveness. You still haven't done that much." I feel the words rush through my clenched teeth.

"Are you serious? You're still holding on to that situation. That was years ago!" He brushes me off.

"That situation? You mean when you cheated on me… With my LITTLE sister?" I say flatly and loudly.

"We were essentially kids." He raises his voice to match mine.

"No, my sister was essentially a kid. We were adults planning our lives together. Two years earlier you would have been arrested." I can't imagine what I saw in this pig.

"You're definitely overreacting. We all were adults, and that was practically a lifetime ago." His voice has gotten louder and he's not even trying to hide his annoyance. I can feel eyes on us and I'm really getting tired of being a spectacle in a public place.

"You really don't get it, do you?" My hands are shaking under the table, it's taking everything I have not to fly across the table at him. "You and I were together for years. You had the gall to practically prey on my sister, take her to Florida with you, and then still come back and attempt to patch things with me. Does she know you tried to fuck me when you guys got back?"

Even through Andrew's dark skin, I can see his cheeks flare hot. "That is NOT what happened." He whisper-yells across the table. I realize my voice was louder than it needed to be, and a table of college girls are giving us looks from a booth to the right.

"That is *exactly* what happened. You came to my room, YOU came on to ME. I was the one who sent you away. I just didn't know I was sending you back to my SISTER."

"Amber, our relationship was over before any of that happened." Andrew's voice has turned condescending and I want to punch him even more.

"Funny thing about that," I take a deep breath, willing my hands to stop shaking. "You have to BREAK UP with someone for them to know that."

"Amber." Andrew sounds exhausted and it just fuels the rage. He keeps speaking to me like I wasn't there and like I didn't experience what happened.

"No, no Andrew. It's not good enough. You both derailed my life. You got your happily ever after, and I'd love to give a shit, but I don't. You fucked off to Florida so you wouldn't have to deal with the fallout. But I was still here. I AM still here. I was the one who had to pick myself up. I had to deal with my parents as they divorced. Everything was on me. So I really don't care what you have to say, unless you're ready to listen to me, and offer a proper apology, I don't want to hear it! I don't care why you moved back!"

"For fucks sake Amber! You're so fucking selfish you can't see anything else. You have no idea what the last few years have been like for Brittany. We are here because she would not stop her relentless nagging! First she felt guilty, then she missed you, then she thought maybe we should make amends and you're being so fucking difficult; all she wants is for you to be part of her baby's life!" He stands, his hands are pressed, palms flat, to the table.

I swear the entire world goes still as I look up at him in shock and horror. I could hear a pin drop in Antarctica. My own heartbeat doesn't even ring in my ears. "Your what?"

Andrew looks deranged. I can see his panicked expression. "Fuck, it wasn't supposed to come out like that. Listen–" Andrew takes a deep breath and everything comes out in a rush. "We don't want to be here either, okay? The startup I was working for got caught in some shady business. They went belly-up, tits deep in lawsuits. The baby was not a part of the plan. We had to move back, we were hoping to get approved for a condo, but currently, we are living with your mother. This last year has been hell on Brittany, and I am still looking for a job up here. She just wants you to be around, she wants you to have a relationship with her and your mom again, so this baby has everyone around when they come."

"Are you trying to guilt me into this? I feel for you but what comes around goes around. You two fucked people, then got screwed. That's not my fault. I'm not inviting toxic people back into my life because I feel bad for them." I scoot my chair back away from the table because his eyes scare me. He's searching my face like he's ready to rip my skin off.

"Maybe you're the toxic one Amber! I'm only here because MY wife wants you to be a part of our family. You don't care about us." He pouts attempting to twist my words. He sits back down and his leg starts bouncing wildly again. The nervous energy pouring from him is making my skin crawl.

There is no way this conversation is going to continue without turning into a screaming match. I know Andrew well enough that he thinks he can pressure me into what he wants. So I push out my chair and slide my purse over my shoulder. I stand and begin to walk away. It's funny, I was worried about all the control I lost. When I had it the whole time.

I hear his chair slide out. "FUCK YOU TOO! I DON'T NEED YOU!"

I don't even bother to turn to him and the bells above the door jingle followed by.

"ANDREW BRINKS WHO THE FUCK DO YOU THINK YOU'RE TALKING TO LIKE THAT?"

I chuckle to myself as I hear Mr. Brinks shout from the bar. I forgot his dad was there. Some small part of me revels in the fact that he has to deal with the repercussions of speaking like that in front of his dad.

The further from the door I get though, the less quickly my body is walking. I feel heavy, exhausted like I just ran a marathon. My lungs protest oxygen and in a matter of seconds I have to sit on a nearby bench, hunched over with my elbows on my knees and my head in my hands. No matter how much I attempt to gulp down oxygen it's just never enough. The weight of my conversation with Andrew slams into me full force. I feel myself crack, and it feels as though I'm watching everything happen from outside of my body. The tears come fast, leaving burning streaks down my cheeks. I sob quietly, so overwhelmed that I don't know if I make a sound or don't. The world melts away and I'm sucked into nothingness, I can't even focus on my breathing as sobs rack my body.

Chapter Nine

"Hey? Are you okay?" A familiar voice shouts from the road.

I hear a car door close.

"Amber? What happened?" A hand pulls my own from my face. "Amber?"

His gentle brown eyes meet mine; brows furrowed and his eyes scared. His hand holds mine as he pulls the other off my face. His hands are warm, firm, and a little rough. It takes a moment to come back to reality and see Saul kneeling in front of me, kind of like a prince in a Disney movie.

"Are you hurt?" He looks me over to find an injury. He starts lifting my arms and rolling up my sleeves to check. "Is there blood?"

I pull my arms back and shake my head slowly from side to side. "No, dork. Why are you touching me so much?"

"It's getting dark, if there was blood, I'd feel it before I saw it." He looks so serious.

"You are so weird." I can feel a small smile sprawl across my face.

"Not so weird, it makes sense to feel around while looking for an injury, I couldn't see if you had broken ribs if you have clothes on."

"WHAT! I thought you were rolling up my sleeves not trying to undress me." I recoil a little.

"I wasn't trying to undress you, that's why I was feeling around. You're crying on the side of the street, for all I know you got hit by a car! I wouldn't take your clothes off right here!" He yells indignantly. "Wait, that's not true, if you were having a heart attack or something, I'd probably have to get my AED and take off your shirt."

"This conversation is a lot right now. I went through a lot just now and I'm not sure what's happening." My head is spinning.

"Well, before you thought I was undressing you, I was attempting to find out what was wrong. You weren't hit by a car, and you're not having a heart attack–"

I press my finger to his mouth and he freezes. "Please, stop."

His lips move against my finger as his mouth opens slightly in surprise, and I realize for the first time how close we are right now. One of his hands rests on my thigh while the other is braced against the bench seat. His face is maybe six inches from mine, and his lips feel warm against my finger. His breath tickles my palm when he speaks.

"Do you just want me to take you home?" The words are muffled coming from around my fingers, and I rip my hand away quickly and nod. I wish the sun was lower because with the sunset right now I feel like maybe my face is ten shades of red darker than it usually is.

"Yes, I can tell you more on the way. Just stop trying to feel me up." I know my face is tear-stained. My eyes hurt. I can't help but smile. I feel a little lighter now that Saul is here.

"Not many people tell me to stop feeling them up." He winks as he stands and holds his hand out to help me up. My face is on fire as I stare indignantly up at him. He isn't that much taller than me, but we are standing almost chest to chest and I have to tilt my chin to see him.

"Well, I'm not most people."

"Trust me, I know." He doesn't let go of my hand as he leads me over to the passenger side of his truck and helps me inside.

When he leans over to set my purse on the seat next to me I gasp.

"SAUL! I SAID DON'T FEEL ME UP!" I tease him but it comes off brasher than I intended.

He jumps back, "I wasn't! I swear! I was just trying to help! Sometimes, when I'm overwhelmed, I forget to do things. I was just trying to be helpful!" He's holding his hands up, making a show of backing away from me.

"Sure." I smile and wink at him.

He sighs deeply, "I don't know what's happening anymore. Let me take you home now." He closes my door and walks around to the driver's side.

Ten minutes later, I let us into my apartment. The drive over was silent, as soon as the car started moving, the weight of the night crashed back into me. I wanted to close my eyes, and I could see Saul looking over at me a few times but I couldn't make myself do anything.

I kick my shoes off without paying attention to where they land, and head straight for the couch. Once I sit, I see Saul still standing in the entryway, looking around with his hands shoved into his pockets. His face is an unreadable mask, and it instantly annoys me.

"What?" I ask.

He shrugs, still looking around. "Can I do anything for you?"

I sigh through the lump of emotion still sitting in my throat. "No, I'm just exhausted. And probably hungry."

"Have you eaten since lunch?" He raises his eyebrows.

I shake my head. Saul makes a 'mmmm' sound in his throat and walks over to the little galley kitchen. I can see him rummaging around in my fridge and cabinets, but don't have the energy to ask what he's doing. I hear the microwave kick on; stare at the carpet in front of the TV.

"Hey, Nathan..." My body goes rigid and I sit up straighter, looking at Saul, who is now on the phone. "No, I know... no, this isn't work related. No, it's not..." He pinches the bridge of his nose. "Listen, I'm at Amber's... No, I'm not lost. No, I'm not stalking..." Saul's voice takes on a frantic edge as he whisper yells into the phone. "Could you just–I know that Catherine and Amber are friends, could she come over. No, I don't know what's wrong, that's why I thought maybe she could talk to Catherine. I'm not leaving until Catherine gets here. Well, I wasn't just going to dump her on your porch. Okay... okay... Yes... No, I found her sitting on a bench. Okay.

Thanks."

I really want to be annoyed, I really didn't want to talk to anyone tonight. I can't admit it, but I am a little relieved that Saul called Nathan, even if it bites me in the ass later.

Saul opens the microwave and walks around the island and hands me a bowl of ramen with a soft boiled egg.

"When did you have time to boil an egg?" I ask, not remembering him grabbing anything to do that.

"It only takes six minutes. How long have those dishes been in the sink?" He's not really looking at me as he speaks.

"I don't know. A few days."

Saul says nothing, but he looks around, taking in stalk of the dirty dishes sitting on the coffee table and the counter. Without giving me a second glance, he picks up the empty coffee cups and the plate with a half eaten PB&J and walks back to the kitchen.

"You don't need to do that. Really, I was gonna get to it tomorrow." My cheeks are hot with embarrassment. "It's just a normal depression mess, doesn't take that long to fix."

"I'm just going to load the dishwasher really quick, it's fine. Did you put soup in this cup? Actually I don't want to know. It's fine."

"If you think this is bad, you should see my bedroom." I mumble to myself into my bowl of ramen.

Saul's head snaps up. "What's wrong with your bedroom?"

"Nothing." I say, taking a huge bite of food. "This is really good, thank you." I say through a full mouth.

Saul wanders down the hallway to my room, opening the bathroom door first before opening my bedroom door. He walks in and then quickly comes back out carrying chip bags, empty salsa jars, and two more plates. He looks determined, heading back toward the kitchen sink.

"Dude, you do know it's super weird, and a total invasion of privacy to walk around cleaning someone's house, right?"

Saul grunts but doesn't look up from the dishwasher he's loading.

"*Saul*," I look at him pointedly.

"What?" He stammers.

"It's weird that you're cleaning my apartment. Normal people don't do that. They just silently judge in their heads and pretend that it's fine on the outside." I smile feeling both ashamed and thankful.

"I really don't mind. I'm not judging you." He says absently. "I know you've had a bad week."

"That's not really the point..." I sigh, standing from the couch to carry my now mostly empty bowl to the sink. "It makes me feel weird."

Saul freezes, looking up at me over the rims of his glasses. He slowly– as if I can't see him–loads the last dish into my dishwasher. He then closes it slowly. "I will do my best to not do it again, then." He says in a way that is not even the slightest bit believable or remorseful. "I just care about you, and I know sometimes when things are hard, it's hard to keep up with stuff like housework."

"You would be correct." I say. "But, it's still not your house, so it's not really your place to do something. Especially going into my room."

"I see that, I'm sorry. I will ask next time."

"Thank you."

My front door opens and Catherine's voice echoes from the front, breaking whatever weird tension had begun to boil up between Saul and I.

"Hello?"

"In the kitchen!" I call back.

Catherine walks slowly into the space, eyeing Saul in an extremely obvious way. "Hey, sorry, I was in the middle of a shower when he called Nathan."

"You didn't have to come over." I say quickly, crossing my arms across my chest. I don't mean to be defensive, but I have felt extremely vulnerable for longer than I'd like to.

"Of course I did." She says.

"Well, I think I'm going to get going. I work in the morning." Saul's fingers brush against my arm like he's not sure what to do.

I turn to him, mustering a small smile. "Thank you for rescuing me today. I appreciate it."

He looks slightly uncomfortable as he backs away. "Of course. I'll see you tomorrow, okay?"

Without a backward glance, Saul disappears, but I hear him mumble something and then I hear the distinct thud of my shoes being placed together against the wall in my entryway. I roll my eyes and am about to say something.. When I look at Catherine, she's staring openmouthed at me. Whatever I was going to say to Saul dies as her eyes glitter and her open mouth turns into a massive smile.

The door slams unintentionally behind Saul and a small 'sorry' comes through the door. I can't help but chuckle a little. An 'ahem calls my focus over to Catherine. She stands with drenched hair and arms crossed. Her eyebrows raise signaling that I need to start talking or she will.

"Why was Saul here? And why does it look like you were in a boxing match with an onion?" Catherine blows a stray piece of hair out of her face.

"Did you get a haircut? Since when do you have bangs?" I'm not sure if I wanna talk to her about what's going on. I know I should, I just feel so emotionally exhausted.

"Megan said it would frame my face better. Now stop redirecting, you've had so much going on and have told me nothing. I've texted and you've said you're fine but Nathan has had to send you home from work." Her tone is frustrated and angry. I can see in Catherine's eyes though she's worried. "Then you go silent, and I try to give you space, but my boyfriend gets a call from the guy you claim to despise, claiming that he found you on the side of the road?"

"What do you want to know first?" I sigh in defeat and fall onto my couch. I hear Catherine slowly walk over. She sits on the opposite side and turns to me resting her feet on the middle cushion of my couch. I turn my body and put my feet across from her.

"Well, Saul was here. What's that all about?" A sly smile takes over the worry on her face.

"We spent the day together and he dropped me off after we ran into each other again." I shrug my shoulders. If I didn't have drinks with Andrew I'd be laughing and blushing over my day with Saul. I can't muster up enough emotional energy to.

"I thought you hated Saul?" Catherine's jaw drops to her knees.

"I did." I pull my knees up to my chest and rest my head on them.

"So are you going to elaborate more or just mope until I go away?" She prods me with her foot. "Because I think we both know I won't be leaving any time soon."

I smile a little. "I did hate him. I don't know. This morning we ran into each other at The Grove, and he looked like... well, THAT." I motion vaguely toward the door.

"I noticed some pretty interesting attire. But I can't say I'm super familiar with what he looks like normally. I know he usually goes for a more business–"

"SWEATER VESTS." I cut her off. "He wears sweater vests. And this

morning he had a NOSE RING. And wavy soft boy emo vibes hair. And...
And... HE TOOK ME TO AMISH COUNTRY."

Catherine throws her head back and laughs. "Amish country?
Really?"

"We made candles!" I bury my face in my knees and groan. "And he
told me a ton of interesting facts about candles, and then he made me go
to his house so he could do his laundry, but we went to lunch after. And it
was just a really weird day, he doesn't suck nearly as much as he seems to."

"OHMYGOD you LIKE HIM!" Catherine exclaims.

"I do not! I just am surprised by him. He's nothing like he seems, you
know? I feel like the person he is at work made no sense when I spent
time with him today." I shift to lay down and Catherine unfolds her knees
so my head rests in her lap. "I guess I just feel odd because I did enjoy
today, you know?" I look up at her. "And–don't say anything–but part of
me is interested in getting to know him better. He makes me feel... seen."

She smiles down at me but says nothing. We sit in comfortable
silence for a while, enjoying the quiet and peace.

"You should bring him to drinks Friday night!" Catherine says
randomly.

"What?" I sit back up and look at her. "Why would I do that? Besides,
he closes on Fridays, remember? So that we can get drinks."

"We'll just go later. But I'm curious, I want to know who this new
version of Saul is. I mean, even I can admit, tonight he looked pretty cute."

"Okay, I'll ask him." I say.

"Good. Now, tell me what happened with Andrew."

Chapter Ten

My alarm goes off promptly at eight on Wednesday morning. I roll out of bed, surprisingly I feel pretty rested after last night. Catherine left some time after midnight and I stripped down to my underwear and didn't even bother getting pjs before falling into bed. I slept dreamlessly and am ready to get back to my normal schedule.

As I shower, I tell myself that this is going to be better. Nothing can get worse. Everyone has said their bit, and it's time to move on. I can get my life back on track, and I'm even kind of excited to see Saul today. I wonder how things will be different now that I know him a little outside of work.

Just to prove today is going to be better, I put on my favorite flowy dress. It's a lavender peasant dress with fluffy sleeves that puff out and gather back in around my elbows. The back has a corset tie that ends in a delicate little bow. It makes me feel like a fairy princess. I pull my hair up in a bun, and put on my yellow converse. Before leaving the house, I trade my wallet out of the fuzzy black purse from yesterday and get a tiny tinker bell green iridescent backpack from my purse box by the door.

It's eight fifty when I walk in the front doors of the library with my iced coffee in hand. I head straight for Nathan's office like usual, stowing my purse under the front desk as I pass. His office is on the third floor with all the old filing systems and old text books that no one uses anymore. There is also a media room up there that allows you to play through old news films, and flip through old pictures of newspapers.

It's pretty drab. I take the stairs, the old red carpet is stained a brown color and trampled flat. The third floor has the best carpet of the entire space, and the mahogany bookshelves make me believe that at one time this library was truly grand. I can imagine it looking like a book-filled ballroom with dark wood accents and blood red carpets. It sounds like something from Beauty and the Beast; or maybe Hogwarts. I stare at a landscape picture for a moment, willing it to move.

"Hey, you're here a few minutes early." Nathan pokes his head out of the office and stares at me quizzically. "What are you looking at?"

"Oh, just waiting to see if any portals open into another world." I head toward his office and he steps aside as I step in. "What's on the schedule for today?"

Nathan steps over to his coffee pot nestled in the corner and pours himself a cup. He looks back at me like he's making sure I have something before he sits down. He should know by now, though, that I don't drink his mass market crap. If the coffee isn't sweet enough to cause cavities, I don't want it. And no matter what he and Catherine say, vanilla creamer, or milk and sugar just doesn't cut it.

"We don't have a ton today. Someone wants one of the big confer-ence rooms for the weekend, so we need to move the overflow stuff out of there and vacuum. Also there's a pretty big stack of books from the study rooms downstairs that needs to be reshelved."

"Perfect! I'll tackle the books first!" I say with a grin.

Nathan stares at me for a long moment, raising an eyebrow. "Did you have anything extra with your coffee this morning? You seem a little... wired."

I roll my eyes, "No Dad, I'm just happy to be back to work and back to normal."

Nathan gives me another look before nodding. "Alright, well, Saul will be in around ten, so I'll be down at the study room desk until then" Something about the way he's looking at me sets me on edge, like he's waiting for something to happen. I hate it.

"Roger that!" I mock salute him and turn with my coffee to find the nearest book carts.

The first cart is on the second floor. I look at the first few books and head down the long windowed wall toward the back of the giant stacks of books. There are small study tables, and fluffy reading chairs scattered down the wall full of windows. My stomach rolls uncomfortably remembering a few years ago when things first went south with Andrew. Nathan had found me sitting, he offered advice and a job. I don't know where I would have ended up if that hadn't happened.

I shake off the old memories and make it all the way to the back. I lose myself stacking books back on shelves. There's something hypnotic about looking for the space each book goes. The second floor shelving goes so quickly and before I know it I'm taking the empty cart downstairs. I drop the empty cart off by the front desk so that I can load it as people return books through the rest of today.

I go in search of the next cart that Nathan has stashed somewhere on the first floor. I find it by the literature and art section and head toward the back of the isles so that I can work my way back toward the front again. I have to work a little slower this time, dodging students as they walk through the stacks.

I pick up a book from the cart, Art and Architecture of Insect by David M. Phillips. The cover had a large dragonfly in black and white on it. I cringe a little, I know it's not real but bugs are just gross. I have to pull off the step stool attached to the side of the cart to put the book on the top shelf. It snaps open and I step onto it praying for it not to break,

"Excuse me, I was hoping I could check that one out." A familiar sheepish voice stops me from sliding the creepy dragonfly book onto the shelf.

I turn and I'm eye level with Saul. His eyes are almost an amber in the morning light coming in from the windows. His eyelashes look like flicks of flame as the light bounces off them. I can't help but note the dusting of freckles across his cheeks as his face is only a few inches from my own. I feel my face flush, embarrassment, I don't know why.

"Hi." I pull the book close to my chest, to give any amount of distance between us.

"Uh, Hi, can I have that?" Saul is in his usual nerdy work 'uniform' he's created for himself.

"Oh, yeah sure, but would you mind." I use my hand to air nudge him out of my way.

"I'm sorry, spacial awareness isn't my strong point." He takes a step back.

I go to step down and my heel catches on the back of the stool. I feel myself start to tumble. I reach out but realize I have to throw the book to save myself. My reaction time is too slow, and I'm gonna fall flat on my face in front of Saul. Then two arms suddenly slide under mine in mid fall.

"Woah, careful." Saul says as he pulls me up into his chest. It's warm and his body is hard like underneath the brown and orange sweater vest is a body builder. I can hear his heartbeat, it's slow and calming. I want to nuzzle in and... I've been in his arms too long, this is weird, this is bordering a long intense hug territory. I pull myself away from his chest begrudgingly.

"Ha, thanks for the save! My knight in shining armor as always." I may sound like I'm teasing but at this point he's saved me more than once.

"Are you feeling better?" He reaches and brushes a stray strand of my hair behind my ear. Lightning shoots through my body as he touches me so gently.

"So much better!" I smatter a huge grin across my face. Fake it till ya make it as my dad says.

"Are you sure?" He raises an eyebrow that had been hiding behind his frames.

"Of course! I mean it's time to start back to the norm. Gettin' coffee, organizing books, and saying wacky things that's me!" He looks at me doubting everything I've said. He stops pressing the issue. I feel wired, like the coffee went straight to my anxiety and the jittery energy is not meshing well with the lovely morning light of the library.

"So can I have that book?" He reaches for it and I hand it to him.

"What do you need that for?" I'm not ready for our conversation to end.

"Oh, I have some of my entomology students coming in for a cram session. I like to offer a study session with me before midterms." He says flipping through the pages.

`"Wait, your students? I thought you were just a study aide here?" I thought he was part time at the university library. What else does he do?

"Well I'm only an adjunct instructor. I offer an intro class to entomology in the spring. That leaves me more time the rest of the year to focus on my business." Saul opens his mouth to say something when we both hear...

"AAAAMBER!" a shrill angry female voice calls.

"I don't think your friend knows you're not supposed to yell in the library." He nods in the direction behind me encouraging me to look.

There stands my sister marching her way towards me and she looks pissed. Her hair is up in a messy bun, she has a gray hoodie and black leggings on. That's almost more intimidating then if she showed up all dolled up like she normally would. I wonder how Andrew spun how our dinner went with her.

"You think we can just pretend that we didn't hear her?" I look to Saul and he looks terrified as he shakes his head no.

"Should I go? I can stay if you want? She looks scary..." Saul looks back at what I can only assume is my five foot sister charging at us.

"I don't want you to feel like I'm putting you between myself and my problems. You can go." I feel awful every time I'm around Saul. It seems like he's been swept up in my problems.

"No, I think, I'll stay." Saul says, I can hear my sister's steps at this point.

"What? No you don't have to." I start to say and shove him off.

"No I do, I'm pretty sure I'll be the only witness to this murder." Saul leans down and whispers. "I'll pretend to be looking at books if you need me, yell hawkmoth." Before I can stop him he walks past a little and starts pretending to browse books.

"Hawkmoth?" What is he even talking about?

"Amber!" Brittany shouts to get my attention.

"I'm right here, you don't need to keep yelling." My ears ring a bit after her yelling right next to me. I turn to face her. "This is a *library*, after all. You're being rude." Her perfect ivory skin is now flushed red with anger.

Her perfect platinum blonde hair is disheveled, and her eyes are bluer than ever like she's been crying. "How dare you, your obsession with my husband needs to stop." She hisses at me.

"Brittany, I'm not going to have this discussion. I'm at work." Play it cool Amber.

"You are having this discussion NOW!" She stomps her foot and sounds like a toddler again. "You and my husband went out behind my back! Then YOU humiliated him in front of the whole bar INCLUDING HIS FATHER!"

"Hold up, let's get the facts straight. Your husband humiliated himself. He screamed at me in the middle of the bar." Of course, Andrew is pitting us against each other; it's his favorite pastime.

"AFTER you mocked him and I. Of course he's going to lash out if you call him and the person he loves TOXIC!" She steps forward to get in my face.

"You're literally screaming at me at my place of work. How is that not toxic?" I can feel panic rising up in my chest threatening to turn the coffee sour in my stomach. I use the calm in my voice to hide the fact I want to anxiously spew my guts out.

Brittany huffs out an indignant laugh and when she turns her eyes back on me, all I can see is borderline insanity. She literally reminds me of Regina George from mean girls. "You are the only one who's ever been toxic. I have no idea why you can't just let things go." She rolls her eyes and I am a split second away from jumping her.

"WHY WOULD I LET GO THAT HE WAS FUCKING MY SISTER AND ME AT THE SAME TIME? WHAT DO YOU CALL A SISTER WHO SLEEPS WITH YOUR FIANCE!" I won't back down. "WHAT DO YOU CALL SOMEONE WHO TAKES THEIR FIANCEE'S LITTLE SISTER TO FLORIDA TO FUCK THEN JUST DRIVES HOME AND TRIES TO FUCK HIS FIANCE?" Her anger falters when I say that. "THE ONLY REASON HE'S WITH YOU IS THAT I WASN'T DUMB ENOUGH TO KEEP FUCKING HIM! YOU WERE NOTHING MORE THAN A SIDE PIECE WHO DECIDED TO STAY!"

"FUCK YOU! ANDREW WOULD NEVER! HE HAD PLANNED TO LEAVE YOU MONTHS BEFORE AND IN FLORIDA HE SAID HE STOPPED FUCKING YOU MONTHS BEFORE AND WHEN WE GOT BACK HE'D LEAVE!" She screams in my face.

I can't help but cackle "HE lied for months fucking you and me. The DAY you came back from Florida he came to my apartment to 'talk. He tried to come onto me and I turned him down. 'He lied and manipulated me! Why the hell wouldn't he do it to you?"

She clenches her fists "BECAUSE HE LOVES ME!"

"THAT'S EXACTLY WHAT HE TOLD ME! WHY DO YOU INSIST ON THINKING YOU'RE SPECIAL? And literally, NOTHING has changed! HE'S still trying to use you against me! Trying to con me into pitying you guys so I'd have to be involved with such toxic monsters? Who would believe anyone who lies about a fucking pregnancy in a fight!" I roll my eyes. "Go fucking home and stay out of my life."

" I AM PREGNANT YOU FUCKING SELFISH DICK!" She begins to sob in her hands. I couldn't care less. "You don't understand, things have been so strange since he lost his job. I just thought–"

"I SHOULD FEEL SORRY FOR YOU? YOU REALLY WANT ME IN YOUR LIFE TO FUCKING PITY YOU?" I feel anger boil up inside me. I turn my back to her and reach for the book cart, attempting to push it away so I can exit the aisle the other direction; a book whizzes by my head.

"WHAT THE FUCK BRITTANY?" I look past her and Saul is gone. Then an encyclopedia Britannica knocks me on the shoulder, making me stumble back. I feel a snap and searing pain in my shoulder as it's whipped backwards.

"YOU ARE SUCH A PRETENTIOUS BITCH YOU ALWAYS FUCKING HAVE BEEN!" Brittany screams at the top of her lungs, throwing another book blindly in my direction. I have the sense to duck and I feel as though I'm watching her tantrum as a third-party participant. Like I'm standing outside of my body. If I hadn't moved, that book would have probably broken my nose.

"ENOUGH!" A deep voice booms from behind Brittany and we see Saul and Nathan standing at the end of the aisle.

"No! I STILL HAVE..." Brittany tries to protest, she's holding another book from the shelf half cocked like she planned to throw that one too.

"No, you will leave campus immediately." Nathan says as he and Saul approach.

"I am having a conversation!" Brittany stamps her foot again.

"No, you are assaulting one of my employees, damaging property, and if you don't want your husband to pick you up from campus security, you'll stop. Go home, Brittany." Quiet red hot anger flashes in his eyes. Even though he is speaking in a normal tone, I can see the burning gaze that Brittany cannot. I imagine for a moment that she catches fire right here in the middle of the library.

My sister turns to the shelf and slides the book on it. I can see her eyebrows furrow. Maybe a second of regret and sorrow. Or maybe I just wish she was. Brittany shakes her head and her face turns angry again.

"Fine, we will finish this later, Amber. Fuck you and your book nerds." Brittany says, giving up and walking away.

"Fat chance, bitch." I mumble under my breath as Brittany flips everyone off as she storms out.

Saul looks at himself, then at Nathan. "Do I look like a book nerd?"

"Out of the three people standing here, you're the only one who does." Nathan looks incredulous, but his body visibly relaxes and I think he almost smirks.

I rub my shoulder, it definitely popped when Brittany threw the encyclopedia. The pain is hitting pretty hard now that the adrenaline in my body is slowing down. I hold it tightly and hold my facial expression flat.

"Amber, I need you to go home." Nathan says.

"What but I..." I try to defend myself, but the pounding in my shoulder is getting louder.

"You don't need to take time off, I'll clock you out when I leave, come back tomorrow. But unfortunately, I will have to file an incident report because it involved more than just an employee. I'll watch back security just to make sure she can't sue us. Call Catherine, she's not at work today, maybe you should talk to someone." Nathan looks at me like a small injured puppy.

"Okay..." I mutter, holding my arm. Nathan starts to walk away and Saul comes closer.

"Are you okay?" Saul bends a little to face me.

"No." Tears begin flooding my eyes. "I think she dislocated my shoulder."

"I can tell it's not dislocated, I tried to hurry and get Nathan the second she threw the book. It must've hit you when I thought it went past you. I'm so sorry, I should've said something then but I thought getting Nathan was the best choice in the moment." I can see frustration boil in him. "I should've stuck up for you sooner, then, maybe you wouldn't have gotten hurt."

I can't hold back and start sobbing.

"Do you want a hug?" He asks, but he is already pulling me in.

I just fall into him and shatter into tear filled pieces.

"I hate her so much..." I choke out, wishing it were true.

Chapter Eleven

Saul gently wipes tears away from my face before I bury my face back in his sweater. He smells like soap, sandalwood and fresh pine and maybe dirt, but that seems ridiculous. I breathe his smell deeply as I try to ground myself. It's calming and reminds me of one of those fancy candle stores.

"Are you ready to go?" Saul whispers.

I pull away and sigh deeply. "Yeah, I guess." I mutter not wanting to pull away from his comforting arms. He's still only a few inches away. I often forget how tall he is. Maybe because he's so gentle he doesn't give the presence of a large intimidating man.

"Can I walk you to your car?" Saul asks.

"I didn't drive, I usually like to walk." I state rubbing my sore shoulder.

"Well I'll drive you home." Saul says, landing his fist into his palm.

"She hurt my shoulder, not my legs." I giggle at his dramatics as tears stain my cheeks. I would love a ride but it seems all I do is inconvenience poor Saul.

"No it's fine, I'll just take my lunch break early. My study group won't be here till two anyways so I have time." He smiles, dragging his thumb across my cheek to wipe away my tears and gestures for us to head out.

We load up into Saul's white truck. I slide in after Saul holds the door open for me. My legs immediately stick to his leather seats. He slams his door close and it startles me. He starts up the car and as he pulls through the air in the truck is silent and uncomfortable. I want to spill my guts, but I'm exhausted from crying the past couple days. I don't want to break the silence.

"Is it weird to ask what the heck is going on with your family? Or have we not been friends long enough?" Saul stutters out.

"We haven't been friends long, but that doesn't change the value I have found in your kindness." I stutter out myself. I guess I surround myself with too many gossips, I've never had someone ask me if they could listen to me gripe.

"My sister married my ex-fiancee. They had been seeing each other behind my back while I was still engaged. They disappeared to Florida shortly after. Their cheating was the straw that broke my parents' already rocky marriage. My mother on her side, and my dad on mine. My dad moved back to his parents back in Ohio. He kind of had always been a shadow in the house. I only really talk to him when he calls first and I drive out for Christmas. He worked a lot but I also was always closer to him. I had to cut off my mom because all she did was make me feel guilty or berate me for being hurt. She blamed me for everything. They shattered my whole life."

"I'm not sure what to say. That's pretty fucked up." Saul says, staring straight at the road.

"Now they're back. Claiming they want a relationship, but all they've ever done has take from me. They are claiming to be pregnant. I don't know if I believe them. Either way I am not ready to move on till they actually apologize. Even then I don't think I could ever be around my ex anyways." My stomach churns at thinking of sitting across from him at family dinners, with a mother and sister who despise me.

"I don't understand why they wouldn't just say sorry... But I'm sorry that this is happening." He sits silently. "What if she leaves him and wants to fix it?"

"Brittany will never leave him. She will do whatever Andrew says. He's so charming, when you're with him it feels like you're his whole world. Till he's done and then he's done with you. He gets bored easily, so he switched majors about eight times before graduation. Part of me wonders if Brittany was the only girl he cheated with. " I sit recalling how he seemed to fall out of love with me out of nowhere. "He'd go through these phases of constantly wanting me to be with him, to completely ignoring me."

"Oh." He says simply.

We sit silently for a few minutes. As he makes a few turns and stops too hard at stop signs. I can't help but wonder if I shared too much. Have I totally put him off with my drama? It's so unfair to get to know him now after years of peace. Now I must seem like I seek drama. I'm not sure why I care so much if Saul thinks I'm a mess.

"What will happen when he's done with your sister?" Saul breaks the silence.

It clicks for me, I've been treating them as one being. One giant monster for me to fight. I think of the clock that hangs over Brittany's head. Ticking away till she's divorced, and possibly a single mother. She honestly deserves it though. Everything she's done cosmic justice has to come at some point. Right? So why am I sad?

"I'm not sure. I don't think that I care." I say quietly. "Sorry, I'm dropping all of this on you. This must be really weird. I can be a bit of an open book, I tend to over share if I'm not careful." I try to brush off everything I've just said. I must sound so horrible.

Saul shrugs and turns to look at me. "I don't mind. I honestly wouldn't ask if I didn't want to know. I'm aware now that my caring or seeking a friendship with you has been relatively one sided until now, but I do want to know you better. The ugly drama doesn't bother me, I've seen Jersey shore, as long as it's not that I'm good. I like that you're willing to tell me about these things. I know it's hard, and I am here to support you if you will let me."

I am taken aback by his upfront-ness. "Oh, well thanks. I appreciate that a lot."

We pull into my apartment parking lot. He slows his truck to a roll across the pothole ridden asphalt. The sting of my thighs peeling from the leather and re-sticking with each bump. Finally, he rolled to a stop.

"My apartment is a few more doors down, this is Catherine and Nathan's place." Saul needs to have his memory check. He just dropped me off last night. Maybe in the light it's too hard to tell where he drove to in the dark.

"I know. I think you should work this out with someone who under-stands what's going on." He turns and gives me a soft smile. "I'm not the best at advice, particularly when it comes to social stuff."

I nod and sigh, "Okay..." the seat has no armrest, so I scoot closer to him and lay my head on his shoulder and whisper, "I just want it all to go away." He wraps his arm over my shoulders and gives a little squeeze.

"I know, it will eventually." He lays his head on mine, awkwardly. "But you need help to make it go away."

"Will you stay?" I ask sheepishly.

"No, I have to go. I have the study group, otherwise I would." Saul says, lifting his head from my shoulder.

"I get it, it's okay." I go to slide out of the car, but then a thought of curiosity slips out. "How do you know where Catherine and Nathan live?"

"I'm stalking them." He laughs but then stops to correct himself. "I don't actually, that was a joke. When they moved in Nathan asked if I could help move boxes after work."

"Oh, well, okay, wish me luck. I'll see you at work tomorrow!" I hop down from his truck and wave a small goodbye as he drives out of the parking lot. I think of blowing him a kiss but then refrain cause I don't want him to take it the wrong way. I'm not sure what way I would want him to take it either. I make a last-minute decision to call back, "For the record, I miss the nose ring."

He chuckles and waves as he pulls away.

I make my way to Catherine's door. It's the same white metal paneled door like mine but theirs hangs a wreath with flowers and spring written in bold white letters. I go to knock but before I do the door swings open. Catherine is in a purple mhu-mhu with sequins around the collar. Her bob is tied up in a sad messy bun that's barely holding on.

"What the hell are you wearing?" I throw my head back and laugh. "It's Cici Junior!"

"Do you like it?" She does a sad sleepy little spin. "Cici got it for me. Nathan HATES it so I wear it out of spite." She giggles to herself and makes her way to the kitchen. "I told him that he already decided he loves me so he can't leave me over my fashion choices." She pulls a coffee mug from the shelf and fills it. "He doesn't have a problem with it when it really matters. Especially at breakfast over the counter."

"Ew, should I just not touch your kitchen?" I shudder.

"Well if it's a problem that corner of the room is safe." She motions to a corner with a barely living fig tree.

"You're disgusting." I mock gag at the thought.

"It's not my fault you've chosen to be a nun for the last few years. You probably have cobwebs." Catherine sticks out her tongue. "Speaking of... Saul dropped you off? Nathan called me to give me the spark notes of what happened at the library and that Saul was bringing you over. You guys have suddenly been together for a few days straight. Is there anything I should know?" She asks me like my mom used to ask me if I was having safe sex in high school. She wiggles her eyebrows at me and smirks when I recoil.

"No, dude. We're just hanging out. He's actually a good friend." I can't help but smile.

"And suuuper cute when he's not wearing a sweater vest and loafers." Catherine smiles knowingly and I roll my eyes.

All day yesterday I've been wondering about him. What is actually going on? His comment in the car made my heart do funny jumps that made me want to roll my eyes at myself. I don't know why it gives me so many feelings to realize he's been trying to be friends with me for a while now. I feel like a grade A prick for disliking him so much knowing now that he was actually just trying to connect with me. It really isn't his fault that he's technologically challenged and I let that get in the way of what I'm realizing now is the start of an amazing friendship.

"SO," Catherine shakes me out of my thoughts. "I bet Cici knows how to build pipe bombs, want to set Brittany's car on fire?"

I laugh even though the thought is extremely appealing. "Honestly, I really just want to be done. I am so mad at how much they've derailed my life already. I was JUST FINE! Why did they have to come back anyway? And my shoulder is gonna bruise" I whine at her. I adjust my sleeve to reveal where the book slammed into. There's the start of a purple and yellow bruise popping up in the shape of the book. I just feel dumbfounded. How did we get to the point of exchanging blows? "I have never seen her like that before. Even when we fought as kids we never physically hurt each other. We may have stolen each other's clothes or hidden a phone or car keys, but we never hit each other. I mean, you should have seen her." I press on the bruise lightly and wince.

"Uh, and you are pressing charges. Right?" Catherine looks at me knowing I probably won't.

"No, I don't want the bother. Life is too hectic right now and I just need it to stop." I pull up my sleeve to hopefully end the conversation.

"Well then, I'm keying her car." Catherine states. Her sad bun is coming more undone.

"You don't even know what her car looks like. I don't even know what her car looks like!" She didn't even have one the last time I saw her.

"This isn't okay. Seriously, you can't let somebody do this to you. Sister or not this is assault." Catherine stands and stares me down.

"I just don't get it. We haven't hit each other since we were like toddlers." I sigh.

"Maybe it's the pregnancy hormones?" Catherine walks over to the couch to sit down.

"If she's pregnant..." I mutter.

"Or maybe it has something to do with Andrew. I acted like a totally different person when Marcus and I were together. I look back on that point of my life and can't believe the person that I was. My therapist says it's normal to have similar reactions to the people we are with. I reacted like my abuser more times than I care to admit. It's called reactive abuse. And sometimes it can bleed into the way you react to others and not just your abuser."

"Andrew is a dick and manipulative. A predator even but he never hit me." He'd get mad and hit something but never me.

"You two didn't live together. Being with someone 24/7 is way different than a couple times a week." Her eyes say she knows from experience.

"I don't know... But they moved in with my mom. I highly doubt that's helping the situation. My mom always pitted us against each other." I shutter knowing how close they'll be. "I was able to forget their existence. Now I might run into them at the store. Or show up at my work again."

"So press charges? Get a restraining order or something" Catherine says again.

"No, it doesn't bother me enough, just like some rando on the street doesn't." I state clearly and sternly.

"Sure sounds like you're bothered." She says out of the corner of her mouth.

"Know what, I am. I am so bothered. I am exhausted. None of this should be my problem. I just want to sleep for two weeks." I place my face in my palms. "I just want to go back to normal. I want to be able to gossip about anyone but me."

Catherine takes a deep breath "So does that mean we can finally gossip about Saul?"

Chapter Twelve

I'm just cleaning my depression mess when my phone rings on the counter. I wipe my hands on my sweatpants and reach for it. Saul did more than he should have the other night, but as I tackle the rest of the mess, I am so grateful for the help. I'm in the middle of throwing out the moldy food in my fridge and trying not to throw up.

"Hey, Saul, what's up?"

"Hey, I'm leaving my mom's and your house is on the way, I was just gonna stop by and see how you're doing." I can hear his truck starting in the background.

I hesitate for a second, looking down at my ratty cleaning clothes. "Yeah, if you want. But you don't have to. I look like shit."

"You never look like shit." He says absently. "I'll be there in 10 minutes." Before I can say bye or okay, he hangs up.

"Okay... see you soon." I say to myself as I stare at my dark phone screen. What a strange guy. Maybe I should change just a little. More of a hot mess than just a mess. Yoga pants might suffice.

The doorbell rings what feels like an impossibly short period of time later. I catch a look at myself in the hall mirror and I wonder if the neon green leggings are too much. My lavender athleisure shirt falls open in the back and I don't have a bra on. I definitely look like I'm trying too hard and I don't even know why. I should change.

The doorbell rings again and I jump. Rolling back my shoulders, I walk a few steps and open the door.

Saul stands there holding up a bag. "I know it's been fourteen minutes, and I said ten, but I stopped and got you ice cream. I wasn't sure what flavor, so I got vanilla, strawberry, cookie dough, and mint chocolate chip." He smiles at me and my heart melts a little. He's changed back out of his work clothes and has on a black and white tie dye hoodie and blue jeans.

"Uhh... thank you." I take the bag he's holding out and usher him inside, closing the door behind him.

"Your house is cleaner." He says, taking off his shoes. He pushes them against the wall right next to mine and I'm caught off guard by how normal this feels. Seeing his shoes next to mine makes my heart flutter. I think absently that his non-work clothing style meshes well with my manic-pixie-fairy-princess style.

I walk to the counter and start pulling out the small containers of ice cream. "I've never had a booty call bring me ice cream before." I giggle as I grab strawberry. It's not my favorite but pink will make me feel better. Although the mint chocolate chip matches my pants.

"I haven't showered today," Saul says from somewhere behind me.

"Did you need to use mine? I have a million different things in there. Do you want some of this ice cream?"

"Do you want me to take a shower?"

I turn to him, and his face is flushed bright red.

"Uh, if you want to? I mean, you can just wait till you get home after this?" Is this about a shower?

"I'm sorry, I need actual consent before anything happens. You seem unsure." He takes a step away from me, back into the hallway. I study his face. His glasses have slipped ever so slightly down the bridge of his nose so that he has to tilt his chin up the smallest bit to look at me squarely through the lenses. It adds to his look of confusion and makes him seem much younger than he is.

"Consent? I gave consent to use my shower? Wait, are we talking about the same thing?" I cock my head to the side.

"Are we talking about the same thing? Hold on, you said this was a booty call. I wasn't aware that was what's happening. I'm not arguing or anything. I mean, I find you extremely attractive. And, I know you've had a bad few days. If you need a release, that's fine. I am just trying to figure out if you need me to shower or not." He stumbles over his words, looking anywhere but my face in a way that makes what he said even more uncomfortable.

"WHAT? YOU, YOU CALLED ME!" I Squeak out.

"I know! That's why I'm so confused! But I can't tell if someone is coming onto me, so I don't know what's happening! I promise I was just trying to bring you ice cream and then I panicked when you told me to shower!"

"BECAUSE YOU SAID YOU NEEDED ONE!"

"ONLY BECAUSE YOU SAID THIS WAS A BOOTY CALL!" His eyes are wild as he looks at me. He pushes his glasses all the way back up on his face and takes an overly deep breath through his nose, closing his eyes. But I can't seem to control the pitch or volume of my voice quite yet as my mind races back through our conversation to see where things went wrong.

"I WAS JOKING! I HAVEN'T HAD SEX IN FIVE YEARS MY HYMENS PROBABLY GROWN BACK!" Only after I utter the word 'hymen', do I find control again. I gasp and throw my hands over my mouth like I can catch the words before they make it across my kitchen. Then, I will myself to catch on fire so that I don't have to deal with the bone deep mortification creeping up my spine.

"Technically, your hymen probably wasn't intact the first time you had sex. Most girls accidentally tear theirs playing on the playground or wiping too hard, or masturbating as children. That is assuming it hasn't dissolved on its own, especially if you'd been menstruating for a few years. Also, if you were relaxed enough your first time, you wouldn't have done any damage." But then he pauses and looks at me, confused. "Wait, it's been five years?"

"I...I..." I can't help but stammer. Saul wants to have sex with me?

Wait, he thinks I'm extremely attractive? "HOW ARE YOU SO SMART YET SO DUMB!" Do I want to have sex with Saul? DO I FIND HIM EXTREMELY ATTRACTIVE? I am too hot and bothered right now to deny it. I have a thing for fucking SAUL. My skin is on fire and I want to shrivel under his intense stare. It's like he's piecing everything together as he stares at me, and I don't know how to handle everything that just happened in the last five minutes. I wish I had a time machine so that I could keep my random word vomit to myself. Saul... Finds me extremely attractive. When was the last time anyone said they even thought I was the normal amount of attractive? The gravity of his willingness to do something like turn this into a booty call in the first place has me reeling. And I desperately hate the fact that my brain keeps saying booty call, booty call, booty call. Okay, focus, neither of us has said anything. He was willing to offer me... release... What the hell does that even mean? And why do I desperately want to drag him to my couch and find out? I place my hands over my burning cheeks, hoping to cool them.

"Sorry, that was too much. Can we pretend this didn't happen? I misread everything. That's my fault. I promise I was just trying to drop off ice cream and make you feel better. I didn't plan on making you feel better... Like that."

"Please, let's do that. Thanks for the ice cream. Wanna sit and watch Sucker Punch? It's kind of my comfort movie." I want to beg him to stay, terrified that everything is weird now and he won't. And I am also terrified to sit quietly on the couch with him alone in my apartment when I so desperately want to know what he would do if I let him touch me.

"Yes, I would really like that. I won't ask tonight, but I am concerned about the fact that your comfort movie is mentally ill women becoming super heros."

"The soundtrack is fucking phenomenal and I refuse to accept any bad-mouthing about Sucker Punch." I huff as I go over to the counter to grab him an ice cream. "What do you want?"

"Cookie dough and mint chocolate, please. Can I sit?" Saul grabs spoons from the drawer. I am surprised for a second until I remember he made me food the other night and did my dishes.

"What kind of sociopath are you mixing ice creams?" I can't believe I am crushing on someone who mixes Ice cream.

"The flavor difference is really nice, and honestly, they're kind of the same because there's chocolate chips in both of them so they both have the same kind of crunch."

"Uhm, that's disgusting. They are two different textures, ones mushy, and the other is cold chocolate."

"DUDE, YOUR ICE CREAM LITERALLY HAS SLIMY SQUISHY FRUIT PIECES IN IT." He says indignantly, snatching a spoon from the counter.

"Did you just 'dude' me?" I throw my head back and laugh. It feels good now that the awkward tension has dissipated. "I'm not sure I want to watch this movie with you." I say sarcastically.

Saul cringes slightly, "sorry, I didn't mean to yell."

"No, I was joking... I think from now on I'll state when I'm joking." I grab his hand, leading him to the couch and shove him to his seat. The amount of touching we have done over the last few days all comes rushing back to me as my hand lingers in his and his clean smell hits me. I yank my hand out of his and sit on it, trying to focus my brain on anything else.

"Why is your face like that? Are you okay? You look overheated." Saul's hand lays on the open space between us and I look at it like it might bite me.

"I'm not! That's just my uh, thinking face." I am a bigger idiot than him.

"I've worked with you for almost a year now, I've never seen your thinking face like that. You look flustered, like you're turned on."

"HOW WOULD YOU KNOW?" If it's possible, my cheeks are even hotter than before. I wonder if I'm singing the couch cushions under me.

"I remember the way you looked when you went through that phase of reading smut on your phone. You're not good at hiding your facial expressions." He gives me a look that I don't understand. I think he might be attempting to hide a smile. The corner of his mouth keeps threatening to turn up and that damn dimple is showing.

"NO, I'm just overheated, like you said." Oh god this is why I can never play poker.

"You barely have clothes on. I can see your entire back and your nipples through your shirt. Which is another sign of being turned on." He looks down, and it feels like a physical caress across my body. My breath gets caught in my throat for a minute as I attempt to find my voice. This is so embarrassing.

"Why are you looking at my nipples?" I instinctively cover them.

"Well, they're pretty obvious in that shirt, and I am a guy, it's hard not to look. But you have really nice nipples... if that makes you feel better."

"Uh, yes and no. I thought we were making this less weird. Somehow, we're making it weirder." I swallow hard and reach for the spoon and the strawberry ice cream. I wonder if I'll ever be able to look at strawberry ice cream again without thinking about Saul looking at my nipples.

"You started it by making your sex eyes at me!" Saul takes a deep breath. "Listen. I am not here to fuck you. On a different night, with your consent, I would. But I promise, I am not here to make a move, I am basically incapable of misreading the situation to assume sex, so rest assured, I am here STRICTLY as a friend. I am here because I do really like you, and I know you had a bad day and I figured ice cream would help. I don't want any favors, I don't expect anything in return." He pauses. "And, if it makes you feel better, I can promise I won't touch you even if you begged me. Tonight is not the night for that."

"I..." I am dumbstruck, what is even happening? "I am not someone who begs for sex..."

"Well, not yet, you're not. But there are firsts for everything." Saul winks at me. HE FUCKING WINKS AT ME. That's it. God, smite me now.

"WHAT!" I take a deep breath and sigh. "Just shut up while I turn on the movie." Heat pools in my stomach and I do everything in my power not to look over at him.. Now I have to sit with him for an hour and half, maybe I should take a cold shower first... Or at least change my underwear.

Chapter Thirteen

"So, what are you doing on Friday?" Our ice cream bowls sit empty on my coffee table, and the movie plays quietly in the background. There is a safe, friendly, distance between us. It's just the right amount of space that my mom wouldn't feel the need to yell 'leave room for Jesus!' like she used to do when my first boyfriend, Sam, would come over. I kind of hate it. Every three minutes I consider moving closer, but given the finality of our last conversation, I feel like I don't know what to do with my hands.

Saul looks over at me. "I don't know? I mean... working, like usual? Why?"

"Well, I was talking to Catherine. I thought maybe you'd want to come to have drinks with us after the Library closes." I can feel the blush on my cheeks and I look down. I'm getting really tired of my body's traitorous reactions around Saul.

When he doesn't answer, I look up and his expression is completely blank. We sit in silence until I want to crawl the walls. "You don't have to." I say. wWhen he still doesn't speak, I make a frustrated sigh and look back at him. "Have I somehow broken you?"

"No." He clears his throat. "I'm sorry, are you asking me on a double date with my boss?"

I roll my eyes. "It's just drinks. We hang out on Friday nights and I thought it would be fun. You know, spend some time together, in a non-work, non-dramatic setting. Since the basis of this friendship has mostly been built on me playing a really bad damsel in distress."

Saul smiles, "I mean, that's not all it's been, that's just all I've been present for."

Ouch. "Well, either way, will you come?"

"Let me double check with my mom, but probably. Although, understand I am doing this because I like you. I haven't been to a bar probably since college. They're a bit loud and smelly for my taste." He's tapping his fingers on his knee and looking somewhere past me.

"Your mom? Weren't you just there tonight?" Oh no, which kind of mama's boy are you? I help my mom all the time or Norman Bates?

"Yes, but I go over there quite a few days a week. My dad works weird hours and my brother is still in high school. So I go over to help her out or watch TV shows with her."

"That's sweet, what do you do for her?" Please don't say run a motel and hide bodies.

"She has macular degeneration. She had an eye surgery about 4 years ago, but it just slowed things down. There really isn't a cure. She's lost the ability to drive, and she can't see the TV anymore. So I go over and watch shows with her and describe things. She has only black and gray cloudy vision in one eye and the other one is completely clouded over." He looks solemn when he says it.

"That's awful. She's really lucky to have you." Thank God he's kind, probably the kindest person I've ever met.

Saul shrugs. "It is what it is. I love her though. It was really hard to watch her lose her vision through college. They caught it, but there's only so much that can be done. She's already in her sixties so at this point it just is what it is."

"Wow, that's really hard. I can't imagine... Your parents are a lot older than mine." My mind wanders to my own parents. I don't think I could care for my mother at that age or any age. "They got married late. They're both each other's second marriages and they didn't have me until they were in their thirties." He drags his hand through his red hair and my mouth waters. Jesus Amber, control yourself...

"Wait, how old are you?" I mentally try to do the math. If they were in their thirties, and they're in their sixties now–Saul is older than I thought.

"I'm thirty-two." He seems confused that I didn't already know.

I don't know why this catches me by surprise, but I can feel my eyes go wide. "For some reason, I thought you were younger. You LOOK younger."

Saul laughs and I decide it might be my new favorite sound. "I'm almost an entire year older than Nathan."

"So wait, you're thirty-two, you own your own house, you are sometimes a professor, you take care of your mom, and you're single? How is this possible?" He has to have red flags somewhere.

Saul shrugs again. "The autism usually does it."

"But that is what makes you worth talking to..." It's true his corky autistic traits make him so smart and interesting to talk to.

"You didn't think that before last week." His words sound condemning, but his eyes look ashamed.

"Fair point, but I didn't get it last week. You explained it and now I get it." If I had known sooner...

"And we worked together for almost an entire year before you let me explain." His eyes look a little hurt. "A diagnosis shouldn't decide whether my oddities are annoying or endearing..." He says quietly.

"I know... I'm sorry about that. That was on me, not you. I never gave you a chance. I disliked you the second you inconvenienced me. That doesn't mean you're the problem... I am." I wonder how many people I've shut out and missed friendship by being... a mean girl. My perspective on life is so limited when I think of it. I expect people to exist like I do, to understand things like I do, and view the world like I do. I've always assumed that people who don't must be wrong. I had never stopped to think that maybe they just see things differently.

"I don't blame you. It's not like we live in a world that's super empathetic and accepting of people who are different. In all honesty, I get off lucky. I still have the privilege of appearing normal." His tone is flat and cold. Like it's a line he's had to say before.

I don't really know what to say back so we sit in silence for a few minutes watching the movie. The space between us feels like it's slowly getting wider and I fidget uncomfortably. Babydoll just grabbed the knife from the kitchen, but I can't focus on the movie. It's like I catch every third word. Finally, I can't take it anymore and I scoot deliberately closer to Saul. Without looking at me or hesitating, Saul seems to instinctively lift his arm to wrap it around me. I'm immediately surrounded by his warmth and everything quiets. We sit like that for a while. My eyes start to feel heavy and I lean more into Saul. The sound of his heartbeat soothes my thoughts even more and everything seems to slow around me.

I sit up abruptly. The TV is dark, and the only light that is on is over the stove in the kitchen. My favorite rainbow colored blanket is draped over me carefully and a pillow from my bedroom is under my head. I get up, wrapping the blanket around my shoulders. The ice cream bowls are drying on a towel next to the sink, and it looks like Saul wiped down my counters. I walk over to the freezer and Saul put all the ice cream away for me. The clock on my stove says two forty-five. Before I head to the bedroom, I head to check the door and see that Saul already locked the doorknob lock. I smile and slide the deadbolt.

Picking up my phone, I go to text Saul and see that I have a missed call from Brittany and a text from her as well. I groan out loud as I send a quick text to Saul, thanking him for tonight. My stomach flutters for a second before I remember my sister texted me. I click over to her chat thread. It's empty aside from the text she sent tonight.

Bitchany: I fucked up. I really do want to talk to you. Can we meet up on Saturday?

My initial thought is to just block her number and not respond. But I remember what Saul asked earlier, if something happened, would I still want to have a relationship with her? I still want to say no, but I don't know if I'll feel that way in five years. And something is tugging at the back of my mind. There's been a weird feeling. My sister and I have spent the majority of our lives struggling to relate to each other. But we could always be cordial. Everything with Andrew just gives me a weird feeling. Something is wrong and I don't know what it is. Even if I still think he can go to hell, he seems unhinged, and I wonder if maybe not everything my sister is saying and doing is completely on her.

Me: Yes. We can meet at The Grove Saturday morning.

Me: However, if I meet with you, it will be the last time either of you reach out to me. After this, you and Andrew both will need to leave me alone. Respect my space and I will reach back out when I am ready.

Bitchany: I can do that

Me: I'll see you at eleven Saturday.

Before I check to see if she's texting back, I plug my phone in and roll over in bed. I don't even want to know why she's still awake, and I don't care. I drift back off to sleep, thinking about Saul.

Chapter Fourteen

The knight stood at the bottom of the colossal tower where I am imprisoned. The moon reflected off his golden armor; he removed his shining helm from upon his head, revealing stunning locks of scarlet. The cold drifted in my window, blowing my golden hair gently across my face.

"Amber, let down your hair. I have slain the horrific beast. I have come to save you!"

"I don't have long hair, but I have rope!" I ran back to my room, retrieving the rope I had saved for this very occasion.

"Here mighty knight! What is your name?" I enquire.

"I am Sir. Saul." He grunts as he climbs.

This knight is strong, climbing the rope quickly. I know this knight is worthy of my love and body. As he got closer, his gaze met mine. His eyes are a gorgeous chestnut. His freckles constellations upon his cheeks. And he has a really hot nose ring.

"Milady" Sir. Saul pulls himself upon my stone windowsill. He smiles, shining his stunning white teeth. "I have arrived to sweep you off your feet."

"Oh, Sir Saul!" I smile, my heart full, I open my arms to embrace him.

"Uh, can I take my armor off, it can be kind of pokey." He removes his

armor, revealing his strong muscular torso.

"Sir. Saul!" I run to him and he wraps his large biceps around me.

"Lady Amber, can I kiss you?" I smile, which seems to be response enough. He leans in slowly, eyes burning with passion.

"How will we escape from this prison?" I hear myself say. My heart is pounding wildly as I anticipate his kiss.

Sir. Saul pauses in hesitation, his brows furrowed together and he's suddenly looking over my shoulder. I place my hands on his cheeks, attempting to redirect him to me, but it appears as though he's in a world of his own.

"I don't know..."

My alarm sounds loudly breaking through the fourth wall of my dream, pulling me out in a funnel cloud just like in the Wizard of Oz.

"What the hell..." I mutter, grabbing my phone to silence my alarm. I sit up and swing my legs over the side of the bed. "Sir. Saul." I mutter in a breathy tone under my breath, mocking the sound of dream Amber's voice. What is wrong with me?

I get ready for work quickly. Saul always closes on Fridays, so I only have a short day today. I walk to The Grove first. While waiting in line, an image of Saul standing in a full suit of armor flashes through my mind and I have to fight the urge to physically recoil. How embarrassing. I have feel-ings for Saul. That's not the embarrassing part, but who has full fairytale dreams about their crush? I'm a full grown adult. Why can't I have a sex dream like a normal person? It's probably because I haven't had sex in five years. My brain has reverted back to my virgin self.

"What can I get you this morning, darling?"

"I'm not a virgin." I screech out like a prepubescent girl.

Larry stands, single arm raised to grab a cup from the holder next to him. "I'm happy for you?"

I look up, realizing a moment too late that I have said that out loud. My face turns an uncomfortable shade of red and I open my mouth but can't think of anything else to say. Today is not off to a great start.

"I don't know what I want." I say finally.

Larry looks me over for a solid five seconds and nods. "I'll just guess. This one's on the house. Call it a celebration." He chuckles and winks at me as I turn away, ready to melt into oblivion.

""I'm going to jump off a bridge now." I say over my shoulder and Larry just laughs more.

Five minutes later, I have a white chocolate raspberry frappuccino and a laundry list of anxiety inducing thoughts spiraling through my mind. I have to see Saul today. I have to look him in the eyes, knowing that I have pictured him in a knight's helmet and nose ring.

I have a crush on Saul.

I groan to myself as I slowly cross campus to the library. Maybe Nathan will let me sneak out of there before he gets there. I can fake period cramps or something. No matter what I do at work, I will still have to see him tonight. I invited him for drinks. Why am I like this? I want to see him so badly, but I will immediately die from embarrassment.

I finally make it to the campus library. I walk up the steps, taking deep breaths. I will be fine, it was a silly little dream. I find you extremely attractive. Saul's words circle my mind over and over again. I stop at the doors. I haven't had sex in five years. I have gone on two crappy dates since then. How do I do this?

The doors open to two young freshmen holding hands, looking a little disheveled. Gross, they probably came to the library to hook up. I walk through the doors. What if Saul and I hook up? Oh god I what if I'm horrible? He's had way more partners than me. I bump into a large mass.

"Oh sorry." The mass is Nathan in a tan suit coat and jeans.

"Woah, head in the clouds Amber?" He smirks and tilts his head.

"No, I am right on earth, ha, in the library. Definitely not a tower in the clouds." I am a terrible liar.

"Alright... I'm not going to ask. We're still getting drinks tonight?"

"Yep." I shoot Nathan finger guns and run away so that I don't say any more stupid or incriminating things. Luckily, the rest of the day passes without consequence and somehow Saul and I don't pass each other at work. Before I know it, I'm headed home without any more embarrassing moments.

I grab my bag and head home, but I've barely stepped out of the library before my phone rings. I check the caller ID and it says mom. My heart jumps into my throat and I debate just declining the call and sending her to voicemail. At the last possible second, I hit accept.

"Hey mom."

"Hi Ducky! I haven't talked to you in a few weeks. I'm just checking in." My mom sounds like a greeter at Walmart.

"I know, it's been a while." Because last time was a nasty voicemail and the time before that was my birthday. My mother and I rarely have anything to say to each other. When I was younger, it was mostly her telling me what was wrong with me or what I was doing. Now that I am older and don't live at home anymore, I just ignore her if she even tries. My family always felt like it was Mom and Brittany against me and Dad. At least when my dad calls, I know it's just going to be him ranting for twenty minutes about football or how the media is screwing with our perception of reality. I normally take that time to do laundry or take a walk. Listening halfheartedly while he unburdens himself. Then he asks me the same three questions; 'how's work, how's school, is my mom giving me trouble'. Then I make up an excuse for why I have to go and that's it.

"Well, I'm sure you've heard by now, but I'm going to have my first grandbaby!" She still hasn't dropped her greeter voice, and it feels more like she's talking to some distant relative rather than her own daughter. "Well, since they've had it SO hard, I thought it would be amazing to throw them a baby shower! It's next month, I would love it if you helped out!"

"Mom, now is not really the time. I'm not even home." I've stopped walking and my chest feels tight.

"Well, Ducky, this is important! We must start planning!"

"Is she even far enough along for this? I thought it was toward the end of the pregnancy that you have a baby shower." I really don't want to deal with this. I can feel myself collapsing in on myself.

"Like I said, I'm trying to cheer them up. This is for the family!" I can hear the undertone of agitation.

"Are you inviting Dad?" I know before the words leave my mouth that this is about to be a fight.

My mother is silent for a long second, and I start to wonder if she's just hung up. But after thirty seconds, I hear her exhale in an exhausted kind of way that makes my blood boil.

"Amber, don't be dramatic. I know what you're trying to do" I can feel her eyes roll through the line.

"You said this was for the family, he's still family, you know." I mutter.

"Why must you always be difficult?" My mother's voice has dropped and is much sharper. She's done with me already. This must be a new record. "This is for your sister."

"Who is having a baby with my ex-fiance. Sorry mom, I don't really feel like joining in the 'festivities'." I start walking again, practically running across campus toward home. Suddenly the sun is offensive, and every person living their normal lives needs to disappear.

"Are you really still on this? Sweetheart, please. This is getting old so quickly. You're really going to be so selfish? Andrew said you'd be this way." Her voice is laced with venom.

"I guess I am mom. I have to go." I click the phone and hang up.

I feel angry, actually I'm furious. I feel tears roll down my cheeks but I'm not sad, I'm just so angry. I have had peace and quiet for so long. I am so tired of being manipulated and used. I will meet with Brittany and this will be the end of it. I want my peace back. I want everything to go back to normal.

Besides Saul, I don't ever wanna go back to the way things were with him. I've been a complete ass. Laying all my troubles on him. He's too good of a friend to me. Tonight is my chance to prove I'm not a hot mess mean girl.

Chapter Fifteen

I stand in front of Cici's dolled up and ready to start. I tug on the straps of my tiny cupcake shaped pleather backpack. My sweater is ballet pink with Pi Beta Phi greek letters in white. I knitted myself my freshman year. We had spent that whole winter knitting scarves for those in need as a project in my sorority. I got tired of knitting scarves and challenged myself to make sweaters for all of my sisters who had rushed the previous fall with me. I wonder how many people still have theirs?

The middle C in Cici's bar flickers, drawing back from the past into the now. I look at my reflection in the door. Maybe the pink 1950's poodle skirt was too much, but it really fit the whole vibe I was going for. Plus it's a perfect excuse to wear my pink converse. I breathe deeply and exhale all the problems that are trying to drown me.

The quiet outside quickly turns into a cacophony of voices after a tiny twinkle of the bell above. Catherine and Nathan are already at the table, but no sight of Saul. I pout a little and head to sit with them. Nathan sits next to Catherine, absorbed in whatever she's saying, but I can't help but laugh as I approach.

"Are you two matching?" I laugh, pulling out my seat across from Catherine.

"I told him to change, but he thought it was funny." Catherine says, arms crossed. They are both wearing the same black graphic T from a concert the three of us (and a blind date that got lost and I never spoke to again.) went to. Along with the exact same jeans ripped at the knees and black vans.. The only difference is Catherine has a red flannel on pulling her grunge look together.

"It is funny. But be careful Nathan; people are gonna think you're obsessed with her or something." I smirk, as if it's not already obvious.

He smiles over at Catherine and it makes my heart warm to see them. I'm so happy they found each other. It is gross how much PDA they do, though. Third wheeling has not been my favorite either. I check my phone and start to worry whether I'll be ditched or not.

"Checking your phone a lot?" Nathan raises an eyebrow and his mouth curves into a smirk.

"Well, it's better than watching you two make googly eyes at each other." I quip back. Catherine chuckles and Nathan takes on a mock offended expression. "I miss when I was the only one Catherine made googly eyes at." I raise my eyebrows waiting for Nathan to challenge, but before he can, he looks over my shoulder and waves.

I turn and Saul is standing by the front door, looking confused and a bit nervous. He's wearing dark jeans and a shirt with a giant venus fly trap saying Feed Me. It reminds me of the rumor weed from Veggie Tales. I have to stifle a giggle as he walks over. He's got an obnoxious pink cardigan that I seriously wish was mine, and his annoying orange watch.

His nose ring glitters as he smiles and my heart flutters.

Nathan snorts behind me. "Looks like we aren't the only matching couple." The stage whisper is so loud and I turn to glare at him.

"Shut up." I hiss.

"Hey." Saul slides into the booth next to me and I scoot as far as I can to make room for him. Except then there is an awkward foot of space between us and I don't know if I should scoot back or not.

"I thought you got rid of the nose ring." Nathan says in a way of greeting and Saul looks sheepish.

"No, I just don't wear it to work." Saul adjusts the ring in his nose.

"You know you can though, right? It's not against the dress code or anything. Amber literally dresses like a fairy princess, the nose ring is the least of your worries." Nathan smiles mischievously at me.

"I know, I just want to be taken seriously." Saul says flatly.

"You think people DON'T take me seriously?" I ask.

"No, I..." Before Saul digs himself a hole, Nathan takes the shovel.

"He's always been this way. He's like a mullet. All business up front, but there's a party in the back."

"Did you just quote Billy Ray Cyrus?" Catherine half shrieks. "Wait, how long have you guys known each other?"

Both of them shrug at the same time. "Freshman year twenty-eleven." They say at the same time. Then they both cringe, as if they realize how weird this is.

"What?" I say dumbfounded.

"We had prerequisites together." Nathan says casually. "I'm pretty sure I was at the party that Saul got it done at. He got so drunk he went into the bathroom with the creepy goth girl and came out with blood running down his chin and that.." He gestures at the piercing.

Saul makes a choking sound. "I forgot about that."

"I'm pretty sure I told you not to do it, too." Nathan chuckles.

"I feel like I'm sitting in an episode of the twilight zone," I say, looking back and forth between Nathan and Saul. "Why am I just learning this?"

Both of them shrug again and Catherine looks as thrown off as I feel.

"I don't know all of your friends." Nathan says.

"I guess. You're just a bit of an odd couple?" Catherine's eyebrows scrunch in confusion.

"Odd how?" Saul asks. "You know, Nathan's the one who actually encouraged me to change my major. We started out both doing the same thing. I figured I could be versatile, but after I got my associates, Nathan suggested I try something else."

"I also told you to stop wearing the ugly-ass sweater vests." Nathan chimes in and Saul laughs slightly uncomfortably.

"I think that basically sums up the odd part." I say, looking at Catherine.

"Agreed. Should we get drinks?" Catherine turns and looks for Charles. Charles, as usual, is making googly eyes at Cici. Catherine makes a loud whistle and Charles comes, almost skipping over.

"I thought you guys were just going to sit and stare at each other all night." Charles sing-songs. "What can I get for you?"

"Two lemon drops, a coke, and..." Catherine looks at Saul.

"Iced tea? The non-alcoholic kind." Saul says.

Saul doesn't drink? Saul doesn't drink and I invited him to a bar. Does he think I'm an idiot? Why didn't he say anything before? Should I have asked him? Wait, Nathan doesn't drink so I'm sure it's fine. Wait...

"Why, don't you drink?"

"I don't like who I am when I drink. Plus, it doesn't taste good, really." Saul states.

"Wait, what did I say that out loud?" My face flushes. I feel so out of my element tonight. I don't know how to date, and being on a double date trying to navigate everyone at the same time is overwhelming.

Charles walks away with the orders. Nathan and Catherine turn around. Silence ensues. Usually, we're not awkward, but we have a fourth person. Catherine looks Saul up and down and smiles.

"Suddenly Seymour..." Catherine sings with a smirk.

"Is standing beside yoooou!" Saul laughs, "I didn't know you liked musicals Catherine." I like the sound of his voice.

"I was in one or two in college, just as stage help. It looks really good on resumes." Catherine has always been so good at people. "What about you?" Catherine says, kicking me under the table to join in on the conversation. But I don't know how. I spent most of my high school years keeping my head down, doing my best on my school work so my parents didn't have another thing to hold over me or fight about. Brittany was the one who did choir and track.

"Oh, I just like all movies. Big film fanatic, you might say." Saul says, smiling. I wait for him to monologue about whatever the movie is, but he doesn't. Saul bites his lip and looks down. His fingers are tapping on his knee under the table like he's playing the piano. I want to reach out and take his hand, to calm whatever anxiety he has.

"What movie is it?" I put my hand on his arm instead to make sure I have his attention.

"Oh, it's called The Little Shop of Horrors. It's a musical written by Howard Ashman, then adapted into film in 1986 and directed by Frank Oz. He actually got his start in puppeteering, but he didn't puppeteer Audrey 2, which is the big kind of bad of the movie. Martin P. Robinson does puppeteer Audrey 2, which is a carnivorous plant that eats people, he does a good job but I think it would've been cool if Frank had puppe-teer'd Audrey." That's my Saul. I smile at him and decide to take his hand, anyway. He goes rigid for half a second, but then intertwines his fingers in mine. My heart leaps into my throat when I feel his thumb graze my wrist. I see him visibly relax and everything seems to go back to normal. It's like everyone at the table collectively exhales.

"Wow, I feel kind of lame for never having seen it before." This isn't as weird as I was allowing it to be in my head. Everyone is getting along, and Saul seems much more comfortable now that we've all gotten talking.

I see an evil smile crawl across Catherine's face.

"Soooo, Saul, got any dirt on Nathan?" Nathan glares at her.

"I don't have any 'dirt' on Nathan." Saul cocks his head at her like a lost puppy.

"No, I mean like... what was baby Nathan like?." Catherine laughs, waving him away.

"I wasn't there when he was a baby." Saul says flatly, but clearly confused.

"Oh my god you're hilarious!" Catherine loses it.

Saul is looking at me in confused panic when Nathan jumps in.

"She just wants you to regal her with stories of me making poor choices." Nathan says, rolling his eyes.

"OH! Nathan always has been a bit of an old man. Like if college was dungeons and dragons he'd be lawful good."

"Old man?" Nathan sighs in defeat, putting his face in his palm.

"There was this one time where Nathan went feral for a whole week." Saul looks up searching for a specific memory and smiles.

"Tell us more!" Catherine and I say in curious unison.

"Oh god. I shouldn't have said anything." Nathan puts his head on the table. "I forgot you were around for that."

Saul looks slightly uncomfortable, but I elbow him and smile. "Tell us more."

"Well, I think it was the week he and Carolina broke up. It was right at the end of school, or he may have graduated. We weren't super close then, but I know he worked at the Library. Anyway–St. Patrick's Day."

"Oh god." Nathan mumbles into the table.

"I know he doesn't drink, but he decided to go out drinking on St. Patrick's Day with our friends, and we met up at the bar called O'Malley's. It's on the other side of town, just past the Meatball Factory."

"Oh! I know that place!" Catherine exclaims excitedly. "Go on."

Saul clears his throat twice. "I don't want to unless I know I won't be fired for this."

Nathan looks up. "I don't want to deal with a wrongful termination lawsuit. It's fine. This story would have come out one way or another."

"Well, we all went to O'Malley's, and Nathan wore a light up shot glass around his neck and we had really shitty Irish whiskey. Well anyway, O'Malley's is known for–"

"Karaoke!" Catherine yells, clapping her hands. "WHAT DID HE SING?"

Saul is quiet for a minute. "Somebody That I Used to Know... By Gotye."

I can't stop the snort that escapes the second before Catherine throws her head back with the deepest belly laughing cackle I have ever heard.

Nathan pouts, crossing his arms. "Enjoy this now, ladies. Just wait till I share your secrets." He looks evilly at Saul. "Do you remember who sang the girls' part?"

Saul looks down and twiddle his thumbs. "Meee."

Now it's my turn to laugh. "No way."

"Saul was actually pretty good, we got a round of applause." Nathan smiles.

"Yeah until you spewed on the crowd." Saul says with a smile.

"No, I didn't. I made it off the stage. I only puked on the sound guy and the three girls waiting to sing that Gaga song."

Saul laughs, "I don't think that makes it better."

Tonight has not gone at all like I thought it would. I look around the table and feel an overwhelm of emotions that I was not ready for. Contentment at the relationships I have with these people, and deep affection for the way they have come into my life and changed everything I thought about the way I was supposed to live. Saul smiles over at me, still chuckling, and I love the sound of his laugh. I just want to freeze time.

"AMBER LET'S GO PEE!" Catherine announces, sliding her chair out from the table. I hop up out of my seat, and Catherine takes my hand to head into the bathroom. Catherine basically slams the door open then closes behind us.

"I need you to date him." Catherine states while rummaging through her purse.

"What? He's just a friend." He's definitely not, but I'm not having this conversation right now.

"Uh yeah, sure, just a friend, as if there isn't chemistry happening. There are basically fireworks shooting off over y'alls head. AND I saw you guys holding hands." Catherine finally finds what she's looking for. "Ah ha!"

"You really think there were fireworks?" My stomach flutters with the thought.

"Duh." Catherine sticks her hand out for me to take whatever is in her hand. She drops it in mine. I examine it realizing...

"You're drunk." I roll my eyes at the gold condom foil in my hand.

"No, I'm tipsy, there's a difference. He likes you and you clearly like him." She smirks, grabs my hand and says "Let's go!" Dragging me back through the doors to our table.

"I don't know what you think I'm going to do with this tonight. We've barely hung out." I almost drag her back to the bathroom to tell her about the booty call mixup from the other night, but before I can make a decision we're standing at the table and the timing is wrong.

"Hey Saul, we were talking, maybe you and Amber should go watch Little Shop of Horrors. Nathan and I have to get going anyway." Catherine smiles but my face feels on fire.

"No we..." Catherine covers Nathan's lips with her finger.

"I want to get in a 'work out' before bed." Catherine says, and he pops to his feet.

"Yeah, sorry guys." Nathan might as well be salivating.

"That sounds like a great idea. We can watch it at my place if you wanna meet me there." Saul says, pushing out his seat.

"I walked... Nathan and Catherine usually drive me home." I stammer out heat rising in me.

"Oh, well, you can just ride with me then." Saul says.

Chapter Sixteen

We pull into the driveway of Saul's cute little farm house and head to the front door. It looks different in the dark. The porch light is on, illuminating the front door. A faint purple glow comes from the window next to the door, which I can only assume is the living room. Hopefully not an alien space transported for him to kidnap me off-world. No, I actually want that. Then I don't have to deal with Brittany tomorrow.

Saul hops out first and strolls over to my side and lets me out. I stumble and he catches my hand. We lock eyes for a split moment, holding hands and smiling. He doesn't let go of my hand as we head towards his door. His fingers interlock with mine. He places his hand on the handle and turns it. Then it dawns on me; I remember the conversation we had the other night at my apartment, and I fight the urge to freeze. I'm about to walk into Saul's house, with a condom in my cupcake purse Catherine gave me, and I have on fucking granny panties.

Saul looks over at me as he reaches into his pocket for his keys. "Are you okay? I feel like something changed in the last thirty seconds."

"No, no, I just feel very anxious all of a sudden." Because we might have sex tonight.

Saul freezes. "I can take you home if you're not up for a movie. Did you drink too much? Do you need something to eat?" His hand is frozen on the handle of the door, like he won't even bother opening it if I want to go home.

"NO! I wanna stay, I just wanna know what you're expecting from this." I swallow, waiting for rejection.

"Uh." He pushes the door open slowly, still looking at me. "I thought we were watching the movie? We don't have to if you don't want to. I have a lot of movies to pick from as well. I have all the streaming services. So it's the lady's choice, really."

I smile. Saul is so easy; why can't everyone be this way? Never expecting more than what you plan. "I think I have to watch this movie, especially if Catherine has seen it and I haven't." If we end up doing... that I know it won't come as a shock at least. Saul will just make it clear like before.

We step into Saul's foyer and my jaw drops. "Holy shit." I whisper.

"Will you take your shoes off, please?" Saul motions to a shoe rack off to the left. I nod, still looking around. I slip off my shoes and wander down the hallway. Bugs, framed bugs, pinned bugs, so many bugs line the hallway. Inside each frame, the name is written in adorable blocky handwriting. I can't pronounce most of them, but they're beautiful to look at. Then I reach the kitchen, and what is probably the living room and I'm shocked again.

"I know you've talked about liking plants and bugs before..." I turn to face Saul, who's standing a step behind me, "but this is so much more than I have ever imagined." His living room is covered in plants. There are shelves of plants lining the walls, and strip lights taped to the top of each shelf and on stands in the corners of the room. They're what's causing the purple tinged light. The kitchen island has the smallest plants in the smallest potting cups laying under more grow lights. Each little sprout is no more than two inches tall. Around the sink, there are plants floating in giant vases of water. Some have rooted and tangled up in the water and some are just floating.

"Where do you grow the weed?" I say jokingly, taking a closer look at all of the tiny plants on the island.

"Uh, that's not really in my wheelhouse. I don't grow illegal substances. I focus mainly on exotic plants." He looks extremely serious.

"I was joking, but good to know..." I feel like I can't stop looking at everything around me. Each plant is so unique. I fixate on some hanging plants that have the smallest little purple heart-shaped leaves. "I love this one."

"It's called string of hearts. Ceropegia, they're really easy to take care of and don't need a ton of light. They also can be purple, green, a mossy gray, and pink. It just depends on the soil and light. I grow the variegated version, which is why they're so colorful.

"What about these?" I didn't even know plants could be anything more than green.

"That's a croton. They're actually super prolific in the south. You've probably seen them at resorts in Florida. They're pretty hard to propagate and take a really long time to mature in our climate. I've had those for almost three years and they're just about ready to sell. They're hilarious too because they have a tendency to faint if you wait too long to water them."

"They're amazing." I study the dark black-green leaves covered in bright orange, red, and yellow polka dots. They're barely a foot tall and so colorful. "I love them." I go to reach to touch and stop myself. "Is it safe to touch?"

"Yeah, these are fine. I don't have anything poisonous. Well, nothing poisonous to touch. I wouldn't suggest eating most of these or letting animals around them." He rubs his neck and smiles uncomfortably.

"What do you do with all of them?" I reach touching a waxy green leaf that's bigger than my face.

"I actually sell most of them. I started an Etsy shop right out of college just for fun to sell some of my stuff. But it sort of blew up. I let my brother build me a website three or four years ago. He manages it mostly, and I pay him. Then he brings me order forms and we fill them once or twice a week." He pauses and takes a long breath. "I love it honestly, plus I've grown to the point I don't have to wholesale any plants or bugs. I just propagate and breed." Saul beams with pride "See all those plants, I propagated my mother plant albo monstera. I'll make a killing off of those plants."

"Wait... Breed?" I look around uncomfortably. "Like breeding... bugs?"

"Yeah, that's what most of the upstairs is dedicated to. Do you want to see it?"

"I'm going to be really honest with you." I take a step back, "I'm not a huge fan of bugs... And it's night time... I don't really think I have the balls to look at bugs in the dark. It's like that scene from the old Willy Wonka... In the tunnel with the millipede. That gave me nightmares for years."

Saul laughs, "are you talking about the one with Gene Wilder? Man, I loved that movie as a kid. Did you know that entire scene was unscripted? They had no idea he was going to say that or get so dark. But they thought it really encompassed the darker side of the book, so they left it in. But all the kids' and actors' reactions to him were completely real. They were all terrified."

"Somehow, that makes it worse." I shudder. "So, moving on, where are we watching this movie? You don't have a TV in the living room." I wonder for a second if he's going to suggest his bedroom. I swallow hard. I don't know how I will answer if that's what he says. Or worse, upstairs to watch with the bugs.

"No, I don't. I have a home theater in the basement." He walks to a door in the corner of the kitchen and opens it.

"Uh, I think I've seen this in a horror movie once. You're not gonna chain me up are you?" I shudder.

"Not unless you explicitly ask me to. But that stuff isn't in the basement."

"WHAT!" I squeak out. My stomach jumps into my throat.

"Bondage really isn't my cup of tea, but if it's something you're into, we can discuss it at some point. Let's just go watch the movie for now, though." Saul smiles at me and my stomach falls to my feet as I stare at him in disbelief.

"I need you to stop making everything so..." deep breath. "Horny."

"Uh, I will try? I wasn't aware I was doing that." His face turns bright red.

"Well, you are making me... Let's just go watch the movie." I say heading down the steps because I can't continue this conversation. His words ping-pong their way around my brain, and I don't know how to process any of it. I think I would feel less on edge if I didn't have the condom burning a hole in my purse. Maybe I should tell him about it. But I can't find the words. I don't know what I'm supposed to be like. Saul is so uncomplicated. It's so hard to remember that his words never have a double meaning. That should make me feel better, but he unnerves me when he so brazenly talks about sex like it's nothing.

"Alright..." He sounds unsure of himself, but follows me down the stairs.

"Holy shit." I feel like every single thing Saul shows me, or every new thing I learn about him is just as shocking as the next. His home theater is his entire basement. The back wall is covered in photographs of him and celebrities. The wall opposite the stairs looks like a mini kitchen with a microwave and cabinets without the doors on them stocked with food. There's a mini fridge as well with a glass door that is full of different drinks. Although I notice at least half of them are different types of tea. There is one couch, two love seats, and a recliner all facing a giant wall-sized projector. The couch is in the back, and the recliner is between the two love seats.

"How much money did you say you made selling plants?" I ask without thinking about whether or not it's a rude question.

"Uh, after taxes, paying my brother, maintenance, plant food stuff, shipping, and all the other miscellaneous expenses..." Saul pauses for a minute. "Probably about nine... nine thousand a month give or take a grand?"

I actually stumble as I step off the last stair. "I'm sorry, what?"

"I mean, it's not consistent. Some months I only make four or five thousand."

"Will you be my sugar daddy?" I snicker before I remember, "That was a joke." I walk over to his wall of fame. "You've met Paris Hilton?" I cock my head at the picture. I move further down the wall, making my way to the kitchen. "Is that you standing with Tim Curry dressed as Frankenfurter?"

"Yeah... I went to a show with Nathan in Pittsburgh. He wasn't dressed up and so they took him on stage in front of everyone and we threw toast at him. After the show, Tim came up to me and Nathan and thanked us for being good sports. He was on a tour of conventions and had gone to that showing. So I snatched up my chance and got a picture. Nathan was pouting, so he missed out."

"That's amazing." I walk to the kitchenette and hop onto the counter to sit. "I've never gotten to meet anyone famous besides meeting the mayor."

"Well, next time I go somewhere, or meet someone for plants, I'll take you with me." Saul says it so casually, and I'm so shocked how chill he is about meeting amazing people. He comes over to the counter. "Do you want popcorn? The drawers have chocolate and stuff in them." Saul steps into my personal space and shoves one of my knees to the side. Without even a second of hesitation, he's pushing my skirt up and out of the way, exposing my calves and knees. My breath catches in my throat and I look at his hand touching my bare skin. But then he pulls the drawer between my legs open so that I am looking down at an assortment of gummy candy.

"Ah, so the sweet stuff is between my legs." My words come out way breathier than I mean for it to. Why did I just say that? I wanna hit my head off the cabinets.

"Yeah, the salty stuff is behind it." Saul leans into me. I close my eyes while preparing... "What are you doing?" Saul asks.

"Fuck." I sit back and smack my head into the cabinet hard enough to bite my tongue. "FUCK."

"Oh God, are you okay?" Saul jumps back, looking at me mildly mortified, like maybe he did something wrong..

"NO! I WANNA MELT! I THOUGHT!" I stop myself, no reason to embarrass myself more.

"You thought what?" His eyes search my face with confusion.

What exactly was I thinking? My heart is pounding at an alarming rate and I swear he can hear it because he looks down momentarily, then back at my face. His hand is still on my knee, the drawer between my legs half opened. He's holding a bag of unpopped popcorn in his free hand and I think I will die now. I have officially hit a new low. Apparently I have gone so long without any type of intimacy or relationship I've forgotten the signals. I've forgotten how to be a person around people that I like.

"I feel like I'm missing something..." Saul says.

I can't look at him. My face is burning. "I thought you were leaning into... but you were really just grabbing popcorn."

"Oh, ohhhh, you thought I was going to kiss you." Saul pushes the drawer between my legs closed and steps closer. "I'm terrible at reading a situation, if that's what you wanted, you should have just said something." His one hand stays on my knee and he tugs me a little closer toward the edge of the counter. "Just so you don't hit your head again."

"I'm sorry. I don't know how to do this at all. I've never been in this... position with someone before." My cheeks flush and I avoid meeting those daring brown eyes.

"Position?" He steps back, dragging his fingertips down my leg to my knee. I can tell he's taken me by exactly what I said, trying to figure out what's so odd about my sitting position.

"Not literally. I just mean… I'm not usually the one who thinks about this stuff so much. Usually I'm caught off guard by what's going on." I feel mortified. Am I really this scared of sex with Saul? Or am I more scared of what sex with Saul would mean?

"Is it bad that I really like that you think about it so much with me?" Saul is staring at my mouth and my heart hammers against my ribs. "But do you think that's all I want? Because it's not. I want you, the stunning, funny, smart and kind you. You are so much more than what you try to make people believe."

This time I really can't breathe, but for different reasons. His hand is warm behind my knee, and his other hand presses into the small of my back. I feel like he takes forever to close the distance between us. Part of me wants to close the distance quicker. But I'm frozen. His breath brushes my cheeks a second before his lips touch mine.

The first kiss is barely a touch, but when I don't pull away, he pushes further. His hand presses more firmly into my back, pulling my body flush against his, and his lips press against mine. Without even realizing it, I grab for his shoulders. Every touch is electrifying, and I want to wrap myself around him. His hand caresses up my thigh, featherlight against bare skin and my knees snap shut around his hips. A shudder works its way up my spine and he groans against my lips.

He pulls back a little to catch his breath. I pull him back by wrapping my legs around his waist. I press into his kiss. Now that we've started, I don't want to stop. I don't want him to stop touching me. His touch is soft yet firm. His hands start to slide up my sides, his right hand moving to hold my face. Saul pulls his face away from mine and his eyes look at me with such tenderness.

"I've been waiting forever to kiss you." Saul whispers across my lips.

"I'm so glad you finally did." I say before kissing him once more.

Chapter Seventeen

"Wow, that was…" Amazing, phenomenal, stupendous, marvelous "… something else!" Seriously Amber, you couldn't say anything better?

"Thanks…" Saul says, running his hand down my thigh. "So, are we gonna watch the movie?"

"Oh, sure." I'm taken aback. That kiss was so passionate, but he's still focused on that movie.

I hope off the counter once he walks away to set up the projector. I look at the wall, which he gestures to with his remote. A large white screen unfurls from the ceiling with a whirring sound. I look at all the seats, trying to decide which to plop into. The couch is too big, if I sit on the side, he'll sit on the opposite side and we'll have a huge gap. I can't just sit in the middle, that's weird. The lazy boy would be comfy but it only would fit me and I don't think I could convince Saul to let me sit on his lap. That's boyfriend girlfriend kind of thing. Which I don't think we are yet.

So loveseat it is. I mosey over to the pleather black loveseat closest to the front and sit. I pick at my nails until the room gets pitch black. The screen lights up with a DVD menu illuminating the screen. I can't remember the last time I watched something not on a streaming service. It deeply bothers me that a DVD menu feels nostalgic. I slide down towards the left side as Saul's body weight compresses the loveseat. While grappling with an impending quarter-life crisis, I'm uncomfortably trying not to touch him while also touching him.

"Are you ready?" Saul turns to me and smiles. The look on his face steals my breath as I nod. He turns back to the giant projector screen with the remote and the screen goes dark for half a second before starting the movie.

I feel myself slowly slide into him, and after a few minutes, I place my fingers carefully on his knee and rub circles. His body stiffens and I hope I'm distracting him; my mind wandering to the feel of his lips on mine. I slowly trail up his thigh, intending to reach for the popcorn in his lap, but he jerks away and grabs my hand. I instantly feel uneasy, like I've done something wrong.

"I'm sorry." I mumble.

Saul turns in the seat to look at me. "No, I probably should have said something sooner, but I didn't think about it. I really don't like gentle touching. It's not you. I just really don't like when people don't fully touch me. It feels like ants under my skin and it's really distracting."

I tuck my hands back into my lap, feeling slightly mortified. "Okay, I won't again."

He sighs. "I don't want you to stop touching me. But here," he takes my hand in his and lays it flat against his leg and applies a slight bit of pressure to the back of my hand so it's pressed against him. "Just, if you're going to touch me, do it like this. Firm pressure is better." Then he takes my hand and pulls me closer, wrapping an arm around my shoulders so that I'm pressed against him. "Consistent contact is also good." He nestles back into the love seat more so that we are in a much more intimate position than before.

I don't know what to do, so I lean into him. His body is warm and firm. I can feel his pecs as I lean my head against his chest. God, I hope to see this man shirtless. Wait.. If I do though... We'll be having... that. Uhm, how do I touch him during that? I thought guys enjoyed gentle teasing. Deep breaths, don't freak out Amber. Just ask, just be upfront like Saul is. You don't have to tiptoe around him.

"HOW ARE WE SUPPOSED TO HAVE SEX?" I say that louder than I intended and significantly dumber.

Saul quirks an eyebrow at me and then reaches for the remote to pause the movie. He takes my hand that I have laying on his chest and intertwines our fingers. "I know you said it's been five years since the last time you did... But the act hasn't changed since then."

"No, wait, I don't mean that. I mean, I do a little, but no." Where is the nearest cliff to heave myself off of?

"I was teasing you... I'm not completely sure what you mean, but I'll assume you're asking about the touching part of sex?" He pauses for a minute. "I think it's a bit of a gray area. But overall, the same rules apply– even if I touch you differently than I would ask you to touch me." As if to prove a point, he trails his fingers feather-light down my forearm and I shiver.

"So should I just... Ask?" I want to be honest. I really don't know what I'm doing. I've been with three guys my whole life. One high school idiot who thrusted twice and was done. The guy before Andrew where it was painful and weird and we had sex like twice before I called it off. Then just Andrew, and that was okay. No one has done a better job on me than me.

"Of course you can ask. Without sounding like a man-whore, you're far from the first girl I've had sex with that might need a little extra direction. I know how to effectively communicate what I want and need. And I'll tell you if something is wrong. Just like I hope you'll do for me if we find ourselves in that position. Or any position." He smirks, like he's trying not to laugh at his own joke.

"If I'm being honest, I'm feeling a bit out of my depth here." My stomach drops.

"How so?" His voice is so calm and unphased by this conversation.

I look at the hand that he's holding to avoid letting him see how embarrassed this confession makes me. "I really don't have any experience. And I'm pretty sure any that I did have expired a few years ago. I feel a bit like if we get to that point, I won't even know what to do, let alone express myself to you."

He's quiet for a minute, his thumb rubbing slow circles on the back of my palm. "I appreciate your honesty." He says, shifting so that he's turned a bit more in my direction, forcing me to look at him. "We have time, and

I have no expectations. You don't need to worry about it right now. Like I said, we can talk about all of it at some point, but it doesn't have to be now."

"Okay, I just feel like I'm not good enough." I sigh.

Saul holds me a little tighter. "You don't need to worry about that. I know you'll be good enough, I don't need much, and as long as we communicate..."

"It's not just that. I've never been good enough. Everyone in my life prefers someone else besides me. Once my sister was born, my mom picked her over me in any and everything. Growing up, I was never as blond or as pretty or as likable as my sister. All I had was smarts, so when I got to college I thought I escaped that, but I didn't. At first, Andrew only asked me to spring format because someone else had turned him down. Then, my sister followed me to the same college, snatching up my friends and fiance." I take in a deep breath. I feel like I'm just dropping everything on him. But I'd rather say I'm damaged than have him find out later. "Then I wasn't good enough to keep my parents together. I wasn't good enough to have my mom pick my side. Now I'm terrified that I won't be good enough for anyone, especially you. I was mean and admitted I was mean and you still want me. That's so confusing to me. I want to be good, I want to feel good and be enough for anyone." I feel a tear run down my cheek. "It feels like I can't be good enough for you, in any aspect. You've given me so much grace I don't feel I deserve."

"I don't think it's really your choice to decide how I should feel about you. And I think you're way better than your sister. She's a little too... loud and bitchy for my taste?" He taps his fingers on my arm in a soothing rhythm. "I'm really sorry that you've been made to feel that way. It's unfair that your parents ever made you feel lesser. And I'm sorry that they made you feel like their choices were, somehow, your fault. But regardless of the situation, people are responsible for their own reactions. Your parents are adults, and it's their job to be emotionally and physically responsible for you, not the other way around." He places a kiss on my forehead, and his breath brushes across the top of my head when he speaks again. "I don't need you to be anything other than who you are. I just need you to be willing to work with me, and talk to me, and listen when I talk. You've already far exceeded my expectations." I look up at him and he kisses me gently.

My heart flutters in my chest with his lips on mine. I'm still unsure of myself, but in reality Saul makes some convincing arguments, and every time he kisses me, it makes it harder and harder to see all of my fear.

Chapter Eighteen

My alarm goes off at ten a.m. Saturday morning. I have an hour until I meet my sister, and I glare at the time on my phone, really wanting to just cancel. Saul dropped me off last night after two in the morning. We made out on the porch until I was starting to forget my sex anxiety. But, as if he could tell I was on the verge of inviting him in, he said goodnight and left. I fell asleep thinking about kissing him. Luckily, no weird X-rated Disney princess dreams this time.

I groan, getting out of bed and heading to the shower. I don't bother with makeup and slide into a normal pair of black leggings and an over-sized athletic shirt. I just need to breathe through this. Think of what I want to say and what my expectations are.

I turn the blaring stereo in my car off. I spent the last ten minutes of my drive blasting my favorite K-Pop workout music. After screaming Maniac by Stray Kids for the last three minutes, I feel like I could fight a bear. I flip down my mirror from my driver side sun visor. I look into the mirror. I say out loud "You are strong, you are smart, and you have value."

I can't help but stare into my blue eyes. The same eyes my sister has. It's so strange, aren't sisters supposed to be each other's best friend? I see movies and tv shows and sisters bicker but still rely on each other.

We never really got that. It felt like a boxing ring growing up. Constantly pitted against each other by our parents. Who had better grades, who was prettier, who was more behaved. Dad is always on my side, and mom is always on Brittany's.

They'd send us into the ring to see who was raising a better kid. Even though we lived in the same house it was a constant battle. Our parents would fight then put us in the middle. I can't remember a time where we weren't in the crosshairs.

When Dad would finally lose it on Mom after days of bickering. She'd leave for a week at some points.

"When is Mommy coming home?" Brittany whines again at Dad. Her hair is in a blonde matted mess from tossing and turning. It's Brittany's sixth birthday and I'm sure she's panicking as it hits evening.

"I don't know Brittany." He doesn't even bother to look up from his book at her. *"Go do something."*

"Yeah, go do something Brittany." We finally have peace now that mom's gone and per usual Brittany ruins it. She sends me a glare that I attempt to ignore. She could join us, but instead, she's stirring trouble.

"But Daddy, my party..." Brittany whines again.

"I told you yesterday I canceled. We will just celebrate later with your mother." I can hear the irritation in his muttering.

"But Daa..." She doesn't even finish her whining before he slams his

book closed, causing me to jump as I read next to my dad on our yellow loveseat leaning into him.

"YOUR FUCKING MOTHER IS NOT COMING HOME! SHE HAS BEEN GONE FOR A WEEK I DON"T FUCKING KNOW WHEN SHE WILL BE BACK GOD DAMN IT!" Dad stands abruptly, knocking me to the floor in the process.

The tears ran down silently on the soft cheeks of the six-year-old. Her hands balled up into tiny fists. Her jaw clenches moments from exploding. She screams at the top of her lungs "I HATE YOU IT'S YOUR FAULT MOMMY LEAVES." Before she can run for it or do anything, my dad's hand flies out quick as lightning, cracking her across the mouth. The silence that follows is palpable.

"FUCK." Dad yells, and storms off down the hall. Seconds later, the door to the master bedroom slams shut so hard the whole house shakes.

Brittany is standing with her hands over her mouth, staring blankly at the part of the loveseat he was just sitting in. His book is laying on the floor next to me, open, face down on the floor. I'm still sitting in a heap on the floor, I didn't have time to sit up fully before everything happened.

We can hear Dad yelling. I don't know if he's leaving mom another voicemail, or talking to himself, but in between angry words there are thumps and crashes. We both flinch every time another crash sounds. My stomach churns as I look back to my sister. She's crumpled to the floor with her arms around her knees, sitting in a tiny ball. Her forehead is resting on her forearms and I know she's crying.

I crawl to her side, wrapping my arm around her shoulders. Why can't she just leave things alone. She knows asking about mom is pointless. She knows better.

"I'm sorry.". I whisper the words because Dad has gone silent in his room and now the house feels too quiet to speak at a normal volume.

"I don't need to be rescued. I don't need you, and if you weren't here, I'd be better off. It's your fault Daddy doesn't like me. If you weren't here, then Daddy would have to like me. Mommy would take me with her because she loves me. It's all your fault." She hisses.

"If Mom actually loved us, she wouldn't leave in the first place."

Dad's bedroom door opens, banging into the wall and his heavy footsteps come quickly down the hallway. We both tense, waiting.

Dad doesn't even look at us as he walks down the hallway to the front door. "Get your shoes on." He calls gruffly, with no other explanation.

We both scramble to comply, practically tripping over each other to get to the hallway closet and get ready to go. Wordlessly, we pile into the car and drive for thirty-five minutes to get to a McDonald's with a play place. Across from McDonalds, we stop for gas and he steps into the gas station. Brittney and I exchange worried glances.

Thirty minutes later, Dad smiles tiredly from the table as Brittany and I scramble through the jungle gym. He waves us down. He pulls out a single candle from his pocket and places it on an M&M Mcflurry. He hands Brittany a tiny pink dog Beanie Baby. He flicks his lighter and lights the candle.

"Happy Birthday to you... Happy Birthday to you..." My dads sings gently to her.

I open my car door and step out. Deep breath in, deep breath out. I stare up at The Groove's large cursive sign. I feel queasy, which will not make a great mix for coffee and scones. Not that I think I will actually eat while I'm sent into fight or flight. I can feel my heart beating in my ears. Each step my feet feel heavier.

Until I swing open the door and the little bell dings above it. I walk to the counter, not bothering to scan the room. Coffee first, before I deal with whatever is gonna happen. I walk to the counter and someone beside Larry stands there. The guy is skinny and tall, and reminds me of a younger version of Larry. He's got light brown eyes and sandy brown hair. Larry has the same smile that he has. He must've had so much business he had to bring someone on to help. I order a mocha cappuccino and move to the pick-up line.

I scan the room finally, my eyes locking with Brittany's. She must've been watching me this whole time. Her face quickly flicks down to her phone. I hear my name called and grab my paper coffee cup and head in her direction. She's sitting at a table off in the corner, away from the rest. Larry has nicknamed it the break up table. It's a perfect spot to end things, in a neutral place with feigned privacy.

I pull out the chair across from her and sit. We both stare uncomfortably at each other. I will not be the first to speak. I take a sip from my cap. I'm surprised her hair is pulled up into a platinum blonde messy bun. Her ashy blond roots have grown out a little more than an inch. Brittany's work out tank top reads Boss Bitch across the front with little black bike shorts.

"Are you going to say anything?" Brittany squeaks out. Upon studying her further, I can see the dark circles under her eyes, and the slightly green undertone to her skin.

"I'm pretty sure you called me to talk." I say, arms crossed, heat already bubbling up within me.

"I just expected a hi." She sighs, it's not annoyed but defeated. "I don't know what to say, So I wrote it." She pulls a letter from her purse and sets it on the table.

"Do I have to read it now?" I pick up the envelope and flip it back and forth.

"No, I just want to be like, a really good mom. They say raising a child takes a village and I want you to be in my village. I want to fix this." She motions between us.

"Do you even know what's wrong?" I raise my eyebrows in doubt.

"Yes, I'm not that dumb. I was stupid and young. I wanted to be you. I lucked out. Everything ended up fine for me. It wasn't for you. I was angry at you for being angry. I felt like you were the wicked witch in my love story. That's how a kid thinks, though. I'm trying to grow up and fix things." Her eyes go downcast, I'm not sure if she actually feels remorse or is manipulating me.

"I struggle to believe that since you assaulted me at work." I roll my eyes. "You got to run away with your fairy tale love story and cared about no one in the way. And, quite honestly, good for you. I mean, I'd probably be tempted to do the same thing if I was given the chance. But life moved on here without you, and I don't know why you've made it my job to fit you back into life here."

"I don't know what you want from me at this point?" Brittany looks flustered. "I'm not trying to make it your job. That's what I'm saying. I'm asking for the smallest bit of space. I'm trying to make things right."

"I want you to let me decide if I want to be part of things. Because this isn't just you, me, and Andrew, this is every part of our lives. We aren't just talking about hurt feelings. You got to run off and start a new life somewhere else, and I watched everything here crumble while also mending a betrayal and heartbreak. You left with Andrew and I am not just angry. I'm mad that you didn't come back when Mom and Dad got their divorce. I'm mad that I have to sit here and subject myself to your half-ass apologies because you're still removed enough from the situation that you're blind to the actual train wreck you left behind. You didn't just derail my life, you broke Mom and Dad because, just like every other thing in our lives, they felt they needed to take sides. And like always, Mom sided with you, but this time, we weren't there to hold them together. You weren't here to help. They had nothing left but one heartbroken child that neither of them cared to deal with. So, where does that leave me? Stuck watching the world burn while your entitled 'childish' self only had room to support her own agenda. And that's how it's always been."

Her mouth drops a little, in shock or to defend herself, but closes it. She bites her cheek and I see her fist clench. Then they relax and let go. "I can't say I would change things." She places a hand on her stomach. "I wouldn't have this if I did." She takes a deep breath. "Our parents were doomed one way or another. They are both wrong, they always have been. I don't want to be a parent like them. I don't know how else to be though, and the first part I think is saying I was wrong. Another is trying to fix things with you. The only put together person I know."

"But you're trying to force a relationship without even asking me if I want one. You can't claim to be trying to be this different person if the only way you know how to get my attention is to attack me like Mom used to. You can't strong-arm me into wanting anything. I'm not a child. I get to have a say in this. And everything leading up to this very conversation has taken away my ability to choose. And you definitely cannot send your husband to intimidate me into talking to you." I don't know what to do. I don't know how to not be angry at her, I have been for so long. I don't know whether I'm being manipulated or if she really wants this. I feel sick as swirls of self doubt swim around my head.

"Intimidate you? Andrew said you guys just met to talk and you lost your shit."

"Of course he did." I square my shoulders.

"I don't know how else to be. But I want to learn and try and not make you or anyone feel this way about me anymore. I don't want my kid to hate me... Or my big sister. You deserve a family too, a better sister, and I don't expect you to ever like Andrew. Just read my letter. The ball is in your court. Pushy Brittany is a child and I'm trying to grow up." She stands up. "I do love you, even if we don't like each other right now."

I'm not sure what to say to her as she slings her purse over her shoulder, and begins to head to the door.

"I promise to read it." I say, looking at the envelope and not her.

"Thanks." I don't see if she looks. The next thing I hear is the bell ding above the door.

Chapter Nineteen

"Hey, can I come over? Catherine's busy and I don't want to read what my sister sent me alone." My heart races a touch as I hear his voice on the other end.

"Sure, that's fine. It's weird you work at the library and need help reading." Saul's voice is a little flat, but the chuckle following reminds me he can be funny when he wants to be.

"I'll be there in about fifteen. Thank you." With a short yep on the other end of the line, then a click of the phone hanging up.

I slide my phone in my purse. Saul only lives a few minutes away, but my body is frozen. I need to digest everything that just happened. I feel exhausted and I barely spoke. I sip my coffee and stare out the window. The sky is too bright for this kind of day. I wish it was gloomier to match my feelings.

I spot a pair of girls, probably no more than five and seven, yelling at each other in the parking lot. They are dressed in matching pink sundresses with their dark brown hair up in a tight ballerina bun. It's kind of funny watching the older one jabbing her finger in the air at the younger one. I'm sure lecturing her for some offense the younger one committed. The younger girl starts to stomp her feet with tears running down her face.

I take another sip enjoying the little soap opera playing out before me. I see their mom pull a car seat out with what I'm hoping is a baby in it, but the large baby blanket covers it. Their mom dramatically looks up and lets out what I'm guessing is an exasperated groan. The two sisters start pointing at the other placing blame on the other. Their mom shakes her head, says something, and walks past the girls who both stare each other down for a minute before stomping behind their mom following her into a store.

My heart hurts watching them. I remember so many times that it was Brittney and I. Bickering, driving our mom insane. I wonder if those girls will grow up resenting each other too...

I pull up to Saul's place as I see him and a young guy moving a large monstera together. They nearly drop the plant next to a forest of other potted plants. Saul wipes his brow as the other guy falls to his butt on the top of the steps to the porch. Saul spots me and a large grin sprawls across his face. He throws his arm up in a wave drawing the attention of the other guy who gives a small nod.

I turn the ignition off and take a deep breath. Then I open the door with the exhale, planting my feet on the gravel drive. I look to the porch and Saul is... Oh my God, Saul is jogging towards me, shirtless. His body glistening in the sunlight. He's smiling so casually at me as he slows to a stop right in front of my door. His shoulders are covered in a constellation pattern of freckles that seem to contrast with his not-so-boyish body. For how he dresses, both at work and casually, he's sporting way more than the scrawny skater boy body that I expected. His shoulders and chest are more broad than they appear in a sweater vest. And his waist slims down to a perfectly toned flat stomach that disappears under his cargo shorts.

I hold back the eye roll at his choice of shorts. A pair of gardening gloves are tucked into a belt loop, and the handle of something–probably a spade sticks out of his pocket.

"Hey, we're just finishing up." Saul holds his hand out to me, notices the grime, wipes it on his pants, and re-extends his hand to me. "Jack is going to be heading out."

"Jack?"

"Jack is me." The dark-haired boy with a baby face waves as he walks over. "I'm his brother. He probably didn't mention me because his autistic ass forgets I exist until I come over to help fill orders."

Jack holds his hand out for me to shake while half looking at his phone. I reach out and politely shake his hand. He's only a couple of inches taller than me. He looks like Saul's complete opposite. His skin has more of an olive complexion. Jack has a stocky build compared to Saul's slender body.

"Nice to meet you!" I give him a bubbly smile, but he barely notices. "For the record, I did know you existed."

"So are you the Amber chick he's hyper fixated on, or what?" He gives a wry smile at Saul.

"What?" I let go of his hand and stare at both of them.

"Ha! Good luck with that one." Jack smirks, proud of the jab he just gave his big brother.

"For once can you not try to belittle me to establish dominance.." Saul rolls his eyes and shrugs.

"You two seem nothing alike."

"Yeah, probably cause we're not related." Saul states, "Did you know, parts of your personality, even down to things like kinks, are genetic?" Saul meanders back to his porch.

"Ew, Saul, just Ew." Jack says texting away on his phone only looking up to glare.

"Oh, so you're adopted?" I ask Jack, but my brain finally processes what Saul says. "Wait, does that mean my mom likes to be spanked too?" I mutter under my breath.

"It was an immaculate conception, you are so lucky to be in the presence of the second coming of God." Jack flexes a bicep and kisses it.

"His parents died in a car wreck. He was a post-mortem cesarean, actually." Saul stops walking and turns around to me. I feel like I can see a physical loading symbol spinning on his forehead.

"You like to be spanked?" He looks like his brain short circuits.

"On that depressive and sexually confusing note, I'm outta here." Jack walks to his beat up old early 2000's civic. "Peace out losers." He holds up a peace sign as he slides into the car. It stutters to a start blowing black smoke out of the exhaust pipe. He whips out of the drive like he's in a high speed chase.

"Ignore him, he lives to make me uncomfortable. It's only fair if it happens to him every once in a while." Saul sighs and wipes sweat from his brow. "So back to you like being spanked?"

My face flushes, and I look down at my feet. "No, not really, I read it in a book once and it sounded fun."

"I'll make note of that." Saul states flatly and starts up the stairs of his porch and I follow behind.

"Anyway... How old is he? He seems a lot younger than me, even. Did you guys even really grow up together?" I wonder what Saul was like as a big brother.

"He turns nineteen in June, so no, we didn't really grow up together. His bio mom is actually my mom's cousin. Child welfare services went through most of their other family, but nobody wanted to take on a NICU preemie. When mom and dad went to see him, they decided right then and there he was coming home with them." He opens his front door, allowing me to walk through first. "They brought him home after a hundred and six days in NICU."

"That's a really long time. I mean, he seems fine now." I can't imagine what that's like. It makes my problems seem petty.

"Define, fine..." Saul chuckles as we make our way through the entry. "He had some delays in the start. His legs were broken in utero when the engine landed on his mom's legs and abdomen. He has some vision and breathing issues which are common in preemies. He's mostly annoying, which is his biggest downfall. Helping raise him and taking care of his medical care as a teen really helped me realize I want kids."

We both pause in his living room. The silence engulfs me, and I'm not sure why. Well, duh Amber, it's because the guy you like wants kids and you've never even thought about the topic. I don't think Saul notices the silent as he prunes a plant by the window.

"Do you want kids?" Or maybe he noticed.

"I've been single for a long time, so I guess I haven't thought about it. I did when I was a kid. But I feel like a lot of things would have to fall into place for me to feel like I could." I shrug. I pull the letter from my purse. "I mean, my parents absolutely hated each other when I was growing up. And as an adult I don't feel the same confidence in myself to be better than them. I can barely handle the childish family I have right now."

"Oh yeah, your sister, I forgot." Saul rubs the back of his neck uncomfortably. "What's going on with all that?"

"May I?" I point to a large bean bag underneath his front window. He nods and continues with his plant care.

"So I met with Brittney this morning and it sucked. She gave me this letter she wants me to read. I just feel weird about it all. She seemed sorry, but I don't know, maybe she's manipulating me. It seems our whole upbringing we were just pitted against each other." I tear the envelope open from its side and dump the letter into my hand.

"Do you think that's the reason you don't get along? You were raised not to?" Saul asks flatly.

"I mean part of it, but she also chooses to be a royal jerk, too."

"If you were raised to be a jerk, is it really a choice?" Saul asks. He still hasn't stopped to look at me. I watch him wander the living room, moving plants around, wiping their leaves, and watering them.

"I choose everyday not to treat her like shit." I snarl back.

"Yes, but she hasn't been around in years. She hasn't treated you like shit in years. You both have ignored each other for years." He says, focused on the leaves he's pruning on the new plant victim.

"I mean, she's alway been shitty to everyone." I mutter, almost to myself. I'm aware I sound like the asshole here, but what Saul is saying feels more true than I feel like admitting right now.

"You don't know that she still has been. If I remember correctly, you treated me pretty shitty when you barely knew me. You just lucked out, I'm autistic and never picked up on it." His words cut deeper than they should.

"That's different!" I feel anger boiling up in me.

"How?" Saul says, either ignoring the rage in my voice or oblivious to it.

"It just is!" I don't know how. She's crueler? She's prettier? "You just don't get it!" I stand to my feet.

"I don't, to me, it's pretty cut and dry. You both have maturing to do." He says flatly, still fucking pruning away.

"I'm the one who fucking grew up!" I clench my fists.

"No, I don't think so. I think you've avoided anything that could have helped you mature. You haven't dated, and you don't have much besides work." He doesn't bother to look up while he demolishes my ego. "Sure you're more educated, but from what little I know, you two seemed to be birds of a feather."

"Fuck you!" I yell and storm towards the door.

"Wait, what did I say!" I hear a shout from the living room, but I don't bother to stop as tears start running down my cheeks. I'll read the damn letter alone at my apartment.

Chapter Twenty

I slam my car door close, mainly for the dramatics since no one is around to hear. I can feel my anger sizzle out. I groan and put my forehead on the wheel. I should pull out of the drive, but I need a few minutes.

Who the hell does Saul think he is? He barely fucking knows me! I try to stoke the flames of my rage, but it doesn't work. I gently hit my head on the wheel. I just yelled fuck you at the guy telling me I was acting immature. Great, really proved how mature you are, Amber, with that move. I feel paralyzed on how to move forward. Driving off would just make things worse, but my pride isn't letting me to turn my ass around and apologize.

*tap *tap *tap*

I jump, mumbling 'Jesus' under my breath. I lift my head and it sticks a little to the wheel. I can feel the stupid mark of the wheel on my forehead. I turn my head to find out who is disturbing my self-loathing session. Saul stands next to my door, his eyes are filled with concern, and fear. I open the door and throw my feet over the side, landing them on the ground. I stay seated, though, wondering if Saul is going to demand me to leave.

"I'm sorry. I should've asked if you wanted my thoughts. I should've known this was sensitive and I-I didn't process how sensitive this sit-sit-situation was." Saul stutters out his finger dancing along at his sides like a pianist playing Beethoven.

My jaw drops. I'm not sure how to respond. I am the one in the wrong. I just can't get the words 'I'm sorry' to come out of my mouth. He looks at me to respond. I can tell he isn't looking for me to say sorry back though. I want to sob looking at how confused and unsure I made him feel. All because I can't handle any damn criticism.

"I heard your door slam. But-but, I didn't hear your car start, so I wanted to check if you needed a jump?" He tries to meet my eyes, but they instantly bounce back to his feet.

I still can't get words to form as a tear falls from my cheek. My body feels heavy, it doesn't want to move. I will myself to stand, peeling myself from the seat. Saul still doesn't look up as his fingers speed up. The single tear turns into a waterfall. My heart races in my chest. This shouldn't be this hard, but my arms feel like dumbbells. Screw your ego and fix this.

I throw my arms around Saul and pull him into me. Even though he's got a foot on me, I tuck his head into my shoulder. He's shaking a little, and I place a free hand over his exposed ear to drown out the world. I can feel him start to cry and repeat 'I'm sorry' over and over again. Tears spill quietly down my cheeks, but I hold back the sob building in my throat. I focus on breathing in through my nose and out through my mouth.

We stand like this for a few minutes. Finally, his breathing calms and he lifts his head. He goes to repeat himself again. I cover his mouth with a single finger, shushing him. I run my thumb over his tears, trying to free him of the weight of the drama I caused.

"I'm sorry..." His brown eyes look lost, searching me for how to respond. "You're right, and I don't really... I don't like hearing about myself, being told that someone sees through me. That I'm not who I pretend to be." His hand brushes through my hair, tucking a piece behind my ear. "I don't know what to do. I don't know how people are supposed to do this."

"It's okay, I don't know how people are supposed to do anything." Saul lets out a soft shaky chuckle. Tapping, gently with his finger to his temple. "But that's due to autism."

"What's my excuse?" I give a smirk.

"Probably your avoidant attachment style." Saul stops. "You weren't actually asking, were you?"

"I wasn't, but if it helps, I have no idea what that means." I smile at him. His fingers dance along my back wildly, but comforting. "But, I would love it if you told me. Can we try again?"

Saul nods, grabbing my hand and pulling me back to his house. We walk up the stairs once more. We navigate around the jungle of exotic plants in pots with our fingers still entwined together.. Through the entry of framed butterflies swirling around us, and arriving back in the living room. He moves me to the bean bag, and gestures for me to sit again. This time, instead of pruning his plants, he sits directly across from me.

I pull the letter back out from my purse, unfold it and stare. I can't bring myself to read it. I see the words but they aren't forming clear sentences. My mind is racing. Is this just a long page of venom and hate? What if it's really a long gloat about how much better her life is now? What if I read this and it just is another manipulation? What if I read it and it's not? My mind swirls around all the hurt Brittney did.

"Are you reading it?" Saul asks, pulling me back to reality.

"No, uhm I'm actually struggling. I guess I feel afraid of reading it." I stammer out.

"Why?" Saul cocks his head to the side.

"What if it's really bad?" I feel sick to my stomach.

"What if it's really good?" He rebuttals.

I stare back down at the paper in between my hands. Am I really this person? Am I too petty to even pull it together to read a stupid letter? I feel my heart racing...

"Do you want me to read it first?" Saul seemingly intercepts my thoughts.

"Would that be weird?" I look from Saul to the paper.

"I am not the person to ask if you want to know if this is socially appropriate. If you're struggling, maybe I can help, I can read it with an unbiased opinion. Though I'm still a little ticked she hit you." Saul smiles at me as a wave of comfort falls over me.

I look at the paper and sigh. I hand the letter over to him. I sit and watch as he holds it staring intently. His brown eyes dart back and forth across the pages as if he's playing pong. He blows a puff of air into his bangs to try to remove them from his vision. I slide myself off the bean bag and scoot myself next to him.

I scoot into his side and lay my head against Saul's shoulder. He startles a little but turns and kisses the top of my head. He lingers with his kiss then turns head and lays it on top of mine. He takes a deep breath and sighs. The weight of our bodies pressing together seems to remove the rest of my fear. I start reading over his shoulder.

"You don't have to do this alone. I'm here for you." Saul whispers barely able to be heard.

My eyes already begin to water as "I love you sissy' appears in the first sentence. My eyes run over each letter and word blurry as my tears start to try to escape from my eyes. Each paragraph reciting her wrongs and her knowing they were wrong. Accountability I never thought Brittany was capable of. The stories of therapy and the fights she's had with Andrew over the years. How she feels like a stranger in her own life and body now that they've moved back. She talks about her struggles to connect with the man who was supposed to be everything and how her adult life doesn't feel as great as she was hoping it would be. How pregnancy isn't what she was hoping for. That it was supposed to fix everything and hasn't. She feels like she's the only one excited about it, and she is hoping that we can fix things because she thinks I might be the only person who's going to share it with her the way she needs someone to.

Tears begin flowing freely as she writes about how fucked up our childhood was. The good memories and the bad. The regrets she has looking back. How she hated me for being perfect. That she wants what I have with Dad, like how I want what she has with Mom. No matter what she did it felt like I was a million miles away. She's scared to raise a child filled with fear of her and Andrew ending up like Mom and Dad. That she can't forgive herself for who she was but wants me to know her now.

"She sounds really sincere..." I try to hide my crying. Though I'm sure at this point he can feel the tears running down his bare chest. "I just don't know Saul, I don't know how to take the high road..."

"You don't have to have a relationship with her. Nobodies making you." He says, looking away for a moment. "Let's go upstairs, I wanna show you something in the bug room?" Saul stands up and offers out his hand.

"I've already cried twice, and I know butterflies are pretty, but if one lands on me, I will cry again." I say, taking his hand.

Saul just laughs and pulls me up into his chest, giving me a slight squeeze before leading me to a door slightly concealed by some sort of tropical tree. The door looks like it's been painted over and over so many times the grooves in the door are barely visible. The door knob is glass, and looks like a diamond and the hinges groan in protest when he pulls it open.

Each step groans as we scale them. I'm sure years and years of traveling through these steps could tell stories that were better than most books. We reach the top of the stairs leading directly into a door, no landing, just another white door like before. Saul steps through and I follow suit.

Going from the dark stairwell to the bug room takes a moment for my eyes to adjust. Once they do, I take in the room. The floors are light oak and the walls a soft gray, the room has multiple tiny greenhouse like tents. My jaw drops when my eyes connect with where the massive amounts of light is coming from. The entire back wall facing the small woods behind his house is one giant window. The scene is beautiful like one giant painting on the back wall.

"Come see." He pulls out two clear boxes from the shelves next to a table along the side wall. He places both boxes on the table. He waves me to come.

"What are those?" I walk sheepishly towards the table, knowing he's gonna show me a bug. I really don't want to see a bug.

"What do you notice?" I step beside him. The lids are frosted and Saul pops the lids off revealing two gross bugs.

"Creepy crawlies? That will crawl in my ear and eat my brains?" I shudder at the thought while Saul laughs.

"No, these ones won't do that. See this one," Saul points to the weird green caterpillars that look like they jumped into a ball pit screwing tiny primary colored balls to it squirming in the box. "These are Hyalophora cecropia caterpillars. They grow up into solitary moths that live about two weeks." He pick one up so I can see it a little better. "I love these little guys, they look so cool."

"Cool isn't the word I would use but I'm glad you like them." I try my best to hide my disgust behind a fake smile. His small smirk tells me he sees through it.

"Then this is Diploptera punctata; it's a type of cockroach. You see all these white little nymphs but a few adults? That's because they've evolved to have family units. They even produce a type of milk for their young." Saul smiles down on his gross pride and joys. "Do you see what I'm getting at?"

"I really can't think right now until the bugs are put away, to be honest." I say, locking eyes with one of the cockroaches, making my stomach churn.

"These creatures both have evolved differently." He says popping the lids back on the containers. "One is a solitary creature and the other is family oriented, but they both are insects. Just because solitary doesn't mean it's wrong, or bad. It's just how it is for generations. Your parents didn't care for you guys, from what I gather about your family. So if you never had family how the heck are you supposed to be a cockroach? These cockroaches want to be in a family unit, that's how they evolved. The moth wants to be solitary."

"So you're saying it's in my nature to be crappy?" I ask, bowing my head.

"No, I'm saying being alone is in your nature, but you can evolve to be different. But animals, bugs, and even people only evolve if they have to or want to." He says, putting the boxes back on his shelves. "You don't have to change unless you want or need to."

"Yeah, I guess that's true. But if it's in my nature and I want to evolve…" I stutter out.

"Evolution is hard. Changing is hard, but it's up to you to figure out whether it's advantageous or not." Saul says as he reaches and takes my hand. "I want to evolve to be better at people, not because I have to but because it's worth it, it means I can be with you."

"Nice use of advantageous," I finally feel a real smile spread across my face. "You're right though… Thanks."

"And even though I didn't say it before, you have already started to evolve. You have Catherine and Nathan. I've seen the way you love them. They may not be a traditional family, but that doesn't mean that you haven't evolved enough to let them in. I've also heard the way you talk about Nathan's sister. Sometimes where we start and where we end up differs from where we–or other people expect from us. That still doesn't make it wrong, no one has a blueprint on evolution, we are all just following our instincts."

"I guess that's true. I still feel a bit lost, but I guess that's part of the experience, isn't it?"

Saul nods. "Caterpillars have no idea why they build cocoons. They just have the urge one day and do it."

I intertwined my fingers in between mine. "I may regret asking this, but I want to see what you care about. Show me all your... bugs."

"Sure, then after that we can talk about sex?" Saul states so plainly.

"WAIT, WHAT?"

Chapter Twenty-One

"What? I thought I was clear." Saul looks at me like I'm being the weird one.

"Uhm, I know the birds and the bees. Thank you. I may be blonde, but I'm not stupid." I huff and put my hands on my hips.

"No, not that talk. I mean what we're comfortable with and what we're not." Saul points to the first tent. "This tent I have is my Milkweed Butterflies, such as Tropical Queen, White Tiger, Jamaican and of course what we think of the classic Monarch Butterfly."

"What do you mean talk about, you just like, do it." I suddenly realize Saul is significantly more experienced than me. I might be a fish out of water. "Also, when did we establish we're gonna have sex today?" Everything else we've talked about so far struggles to stay in my brain as I am assaulted by a wave of nerves and a few x-rated images from my princess themed dream the other night.

"I didn't say we're having sex today. You assumed that. I also want us both to enjoy it. When you don't talk about sex, how do you know what to even do? How are we supposed to enjoy sex if we're just flopping around hoping it feels good?" Saul shrugs.

"I.. I'm not sure. It doesn't have to be... Can we focus on this, first, and bugs after. I don't think I can focus on your stuff thinking about you wanting to have sex with me." I rub my arm uncomfortably.

"Yeah sure I have some chairs by my viewing window." He starts walking to the huge window.

Two yellow modern sitting chairs and a small end table sit between them in front of the window. I have a momentary image of myself sitting in one of these chairs reading one afternoon while Saul takes care of the butterflies. I say something over my shoulder to him and he turns around and chuckles. I go back to my book and he goes back to his work. It's peaceful, and jars me to my core. I can feel a small edge of panic taking over me as Saul sits in one of the chairs and looks back at me expectantly.

I try for a smile as I sit, but tension courses under my skin. Saul doesn't say anything right away, he just leans back and looks out the window for a long moment. He's still shirtless, and I study the way his freckles look in the easy afternoon light. I've never been one for photography, but each dip and curve of his muscles and the dusting of freckles across his shoulders is mesmerizing.

When the silence is too much, I clear my throat and attempt to speak. "So... sex." I cringe at my own voice and rub at my face.

When I look back up, Saul is studying me. His face is blank and open, which is both comforting and unnerving. There is no judgment, but also he doesn't give away any hint of emotion. After another moment of silence Saul leans forward slightly. "Let's start off easy. Do you even want to think about having sex with me?"

I feel my entire body flush pink. It takes me a moment but I finally will myself to open my mouth to answer. "Yes." The word sounds breathy, but I don't break eye contact like I want to.

"That's a good start." He gives me a reassuring smile. "What about protection? Are you on birth control? When was the last time you had an STI screening? Do you want to use condoms? Do you have any allergies to lubricants, or types of condoms?"

I stare blankly as my heart starts to race. "I mean... I'm on the pill." I swallow hard. "I... had an STD screening after Andrew and–for obvious reasons–but the rest..." I stop myself before I start to ramble.

"Have you slept with anyone since Andrew?" Saul still looks obnoxiously placid, but his fingers are tapping slowly on his knee.

I shake my head and Saul nods.

"I had an STI screening about eight months ago. I just did it as part of my routine yearly appointment, it's been about nine months since the last time I slept with anyone. I've never been treated for any infections, though. What about foreplay or masturbation?"

I almost choke on my tongue. "What about them?" I squeak out.

"Do you masturbate often? Would you be able to tell me or show me what gets you off?"

I stare because that's all that I feel like I can do. My pulse races in my ears and I suddenly feel like I've done something wrong by not having the answers to any of these questions. Who knew being inexperienced could feel so wrong. For my entire life I feel like I've been told that if I don't know, then that's a good thing, but now that I have someone like Saul, not knowing feels like a problem.

An image of us, sitting in these chairs with my hand between my legs while he watches me comes into my mind completely of its own accord. I am now too hot all over and aching in places that haven't ached in a long time.

"Amber?" I look at Saul and for the first time, he looks like he might be feeling nervous or insecure, too. After a long moment of silence, he holds a hand out to me. "Come here."

I stand and walk hesitantly, closing the three feet of space between us. The heat in my stomach starts to subside, replaced with more trepidation. As soon as my fingers brush his, he's pulling me down into his lap and wrapping his arms around me. I exhale all the air I didn't know I was holding in my lungs. "I'm sorry." I whisper.

Saul rubs slow circles on my lower back and I lean into his warmth. "You have nothing to be sorry for. Tell me what you're feeling right now." He takes my hand and presses a soft kiss to my knuckles before interlocking our fingers together and settling them on my knee.

I sigh and lean my head on his shoulder, curling into him. His skin is soft, and he smells slightly of sweat and earth. "I feel overwhelmed."

"Alright, let's check in. When did you start feeling overwhelmed?"

"Right about the moment you wanted to talk about sex." I try to laugh to break through some of the tension, but I can feel Saul's body go rigid under me.

"If you're not ready for this, I'm not trying to push you." He says matter-of-factly.

"No, that's definitely not it. I just don't have any answers for you. I want to, I want to be able to talk about this like an adult who knows what's happening, but I just can't."

"Why can't you?"

"I feel like I've tried really hard to forget that I have a body." I say honestly. "I don't think about touching myself, it always makes me feel weird afterward. I don't know if I ever had an intentional... orgasm with anyone." The words stick in my throat and I feel even more embarrassed that I can barely say orgasm. "I don't know what I like or don't like, and I just really don't want to disappoint you."

Saul kisses the top of my head as his hand still rubs slow circles on my back. "You're not going to disappoint me." He says into my hair.

"Honestly, I'm the most annoyed at myself for having so many stupid emotions about something that shouldn't be this big of a deal. It's a normal function, basically everything alive does it, so why do I feel like I want to cry?" I shudder a little as Saul's hand slows on my back.

"I don't think it's not a big deal. Sex is a big deal, that's why we are having this talk. It's not nothing, and I don't want you to think I'm just asking these questions because it's nothing to me. It's important that we understand each other, and I really appreciate your honesty, even though you feel uncomfortable."

The earnestness in Saul's voice has a lump forming in my throat. I nod against him and we sit in silence for a while. Finally, Saul speaks again. "We can take things slow. If talking is too much, we can figure it out together. We can even take sex off the table for now and just see where things go. I just don't want to make you uncomfortable or push you to do something you don't like. So, you have to promise me that you'll tell me if you are ever uncomfortable or want me to stop. I would never let you do something to me that makes me feel uncomfortable or unsafe; I want the same promise from you."

"Do we need a safe word or something?" I attempt to sound teasing.

"If that would make you feel better, we can do that, but I think a simple 'stop' would be okay for now." He smiles as he brushes my cheek with a kiss.

"'Stop' works for me." I turn to look at him and my heart jumps into my throat because he's right there. His dark eyes are studying my face intently, and it feels like all the oxygen leaves the surrounding room.

"I'd really like to kiss you now." His hand travels up my back to the back of my head as he pulls me closer to him. His lips brush against mine and heat shoots down my spine. I nod and he kisses me again, pressing my body to his. When we break away, his eyes burn into me.

"If you want to do more than kiss, we're going to have to get out of here. I am going to imagine all the butterflies watching us, and I don't think I can handle that." I laugh, but I mean it. I know they're fucking watching us even now.

Saul chuckles and shifts so that I can stand. He follows me as we leave the room holding my hand the entire way.

Chapter Twenty-Two

Saul leads me to a door that I didn't notice before, tucked behind one of the butterfly containers.

"You sleep in your bug room?" I ask, slightly fearful that I can't get away from them.

"Not technically. This was one big loft bedroom when I moved in, over time I turned it into two separate spaces." The door he opens is much newer than the one on the main floor, and I feel like I step into a library bedroom straight from a fantasy novel. Floor to ceiling bookshelves cover two of the walls with a large picture window surrounded by bugs, artwork, and some dark green hanging plants taking up most of the Eastern wall. Saul's bed rests by itself with an end table that seems to be built from plants.

"Wow." Is all I can say as I take in the view around me. It's whimsical and cozy and I think I never want to leave. Until I make eye contact with an up close portrait of a praying mantis that sends chills down my spine. Never is such a strong word, I don't currently want to leave..

"This is my personal collection of my favorite things." He says sheepishly.

"It's incredible." I peel my eyes off the portrait to absorb the magnitude of the rest of the space.

"Can I take your shirt off?" Saul closes the distance between us and kisses me. My hands rest on his bare stomach and suddenly I can't remember what any part of his room looks like.

"That's quite direct." I smile uncomfortably.

"I asked a question." The slight growl in his tone stirs something in me.

"Yes." I say against his mouth.

"Lift your arms for me." His eyes are bright in a way I haven't seen before..

I do as he says and he takes the hem of my shirt and lifts it over my head. Saul leans his forehead against mine and looks down. It's like I can feel where his eyes roam; a physical touch against my skin. I feel his breath across my bare chest and resist the urge to wrap my arms around my stomach. Instead, I press my hands against his body. He wraps his hands around my hips and pulls me closer. I regret the cheap sports bra I threw on this under my athletic shirt, but I didn't expect to end up in Saul's bedroom this morning.

He rubs his cheek against mine, the faintest feel of soft stubble sends goosebumps up the back of my arms. Finding my lips again he kisses me gently as his hands snake up my hips, thumbs lightly brushing my ribcage before he trails his hands back down again. I shiver involuntarily, breaking our kiss slightly. I push down the small bit of unease that creeps up my spine, willing the feelings to die where they are. I've always had an odd sort of detachment with my body. Normally I can ignore it, but the way his fingers skim my rib cage reminds me of how little I really have going on. But when he touches me again my brain starts to go hazy around the edges.

"Do you like being touched like that?" He slowly draws out against my lips.

I nod because I can't speak as he does it again. Heat spreads across my belly engulfing my entire body. For a few long moments we stand like that, Saul gently caressing my sides, kissing me deliberately. When I wrap my arms around his shoulders, bringing our bodies together fully he groans against my lips and his hands tighten their hold on my sides.

Saul's mouth leaves mine, trailing kisses down my neck until he reaches my shoulder. I lean into him, finding myself craving more. I want to touch him just as much as he's touching me. I press my lips to his collarbone as he walks me backwards on my tiptoes. When my thighs hit the back of his bed he presses me down slightly until I sit. Then he steps back and unbuttons his pants. My mouth goes dry as I watch the motion with rapt attention. His boxers are plain blue and I can see the outline of him beneath the thin fabric.

When he sees the look on my face, he clarifies, "I worked in these pants today, I can't get into my bed with them on. I won't be able to think of anything else."

I nod, "Do... do you need me to take mine off too?"

Saul swallows hard, looking me over. Something in his face makes me want to without even knowing his answer. "I won't ask that of you. I can always change the sheets later."

I try not to take offense to that, knowing that he doesn't mean it the way it sounds. I scoot back slightly anyway, feeling slightly bolder than normal. I slide my leggings down, sitting back up to push them from my ankles. When I look back up, Saul is standing, his mouth slightly opened, watching me. The look on his face sends electricity buzzing through my limbs and I know I made the right choice.

Saul's eyes travel up my legs, across my stomach and my chest as he closes the distance between us and sits on the edge of the bed next to me. "Check in real fast? Are you still okay?" his hand cups the small of my back waiting for permission. I don't know what he sees, but I try not to dwell on it too long. It suddenly feels so bright in the room, I hope he can't see too much.

"I'm okay, are you okay?"

Saul's expression is hungry as he looks at me. "I'm okay."

He takes my face in his hands and his lips connect more forcefully with mine. Normally at this point I would feel self conscious, but at the moment all I can think about is the way Saul is slowly laying me back on the bed. The way his body shifts over me and settles like a blanket. It has me bending my knees around his hips, my hands grasp his shoulders as I attempt to pull him closer. He kisses my neck again, lingering against my skin and a breathy sound comes out of me. Saul's thumb brushes against my breast and even through the material of my sports bra my nipples peak almost painfully straining against the fabric.

"Can I take this off?" Saul asks, kissing my chest right between my breasts.

I nod and sit up, helping him take the tight piece of clothing off quickly. On instinct I lift a hand to cover myself but he stops me, reclining me back and then sitting up to look at me.

"My god... look at you." Saul's face is so openly full of veneration I actually look down at myself, hoping to see whatever he sees. "You are so beautiful." He leans forward, kissing between my breasts again before taking one of my nipples into his mouth. I feel my entire back come off the bed when he sucks gently, and he wraps his arm around me, anchoring my body to his.

"I can tell you like when I do that." He whispers across my skin, trailing soft kisses on the way to my other breast. When he does it again on that side I place my hand over my mouth to stifle a moan that seems way too loud. My breathing feels way too erratic already.

"Stop..." I whisper. Saul immediately pulls his hands off me.

"What's wrong?" Saul says, eyes filled with worry.

"Nothing." I feel frozen; my body doesn't feel like mine anymore. I throw my hands over my face and take a deep breath. The bed moves around me and the next thing I know, Saul is gently taking hold of my wrist.

"Check-in?" He asks quietly, pulling one of my hands away from my face. All the tension from a moment ago fades, and I breathe again rolling to my side. "What went wrong?"

"Nothing, nothing's wrong. Not like I'm sure you're thinking."

"I'm not really thinking about anything, that's why I asked for a check-in." There's kindness in his eyes.

I roll to my side and study the soft covers beneath me for a long moment before I can figure out what to say. I can't quite seem to identify where the trepidation is coming from. There's a swirl of unease rising so closely with all the big feelings I seem to have right now. It's like my skin suddenly can't contain any of it. I don't even know where to begin as my brain just starts screaming to run.

"I feel exposed." I say finally, unsure of what else to say.

"You can put your clothes back on..."

"No," I rub my face in frustration over not being able to express myself. "I cried a lot today, what if my face is still puffy. And it's really bright in here. It feels really bright in here. You can see so much."

"I know, I like it. And your face isn't puffy." He says quietly, even though his eyes never leave my face, his hand grips my hip tightly.

"I don't know if I can handle how much of me you can see." I blurt out and then bury my face in the bed too embarrassed to look at him.

"I don't think I understand?"

I sigh, "Just a minute ago, you were looking at me... and the way you looked at me, I don't know what you saw. I know you didn't see much." The words are muffled in the bed. "There's nothing to see. I basically look like a boy when I don't have clothes on. It's so bright in here I can't even pretend you can't tell. Every time you look at me I can see your face, and I can't quite understand what is happening. I have so many feelings swirling around inside of my body right now I don't think I could focus on what's happening even though I want to. We have barely started knowing each other, and this is really new for me. I don't know that I've ever been in a position where I want to be with someone this badly and it's freaking me out. What if it's all disappointing?"

I gasp for air, not realizing that I hadn't breathed till that moment. Saul's arms come around me and his lips press firmly to my forehead. He holds me against himself tightly, and everything around us fades for a few blissful moments.

"I'm not completely sure I understand, but nothing about you has been disappointing." He says.

"It feels like every time I go to do something recently, I just don't know how to be a real person about it. I don't know how to exist with the thoughts and emotions that I have when I'm with you. I don't know how to navigate what I want, and I feel like I'm so predispositioned to one type of reaction to life that if I attempt something else, my brain short circuits and refuses to keep going."

"Are you sure you're not autistic?"

My eyes snap to Saul's and I see the amused expression on his face. "That was a joke, right?"

"Yes, although... you described most of my lifelong feelings perfectly." He sits up and motions for me to move as well as he pulls the covers back from the pillows and we crawl under them. I pull the blankets up to my chin as Saul shifts to get comfortable on his side facing me. The fluffy comforter offers the protection I felt like I was missing and I finally relax fully.

"Why don't you like the light?" He asks.

"I don't know." I pause, and Saul waits, obviously not satisfied with that answer and unwilling to move on until we talk. "I've never been a particular fan of my body."

"Why?"

"I didn't develop like everyone else. I've always had some trouble gaining weight, my metabolism started to get weird in my teens and through puberty so I just could never quite keep weight on. My mom used to tell me all the time that I looked a little too much like a boy for my own good, but then would praise how thin I was until I needed to look like a woman for something. My senior prom it was almost impossible to find a dress that looked good and fit me because I have nothing going on up top or lower. The style that was in the year I graduated high school made me look like a pretzel stick. My mom had me put these weird flesh colored plastic things in my bra just so I'd be able to hold my dress up."

"That's fucked up. You were a child."

"I still look like a child." I try to diffuse the tension I feel but it doesn't work, he's still looking at me with all the intensity that he always has.

"What about the rest of what you said?" He asks after a moment of looking me over. I can tell I'm not getting out of the vulnerability tonight so I just scoot closer to him before speaking. His arm rests over my hip and he rubs more slow, soothing circles on my lower back through the blanket.

"I don't know." I look at him. "I really like you Saul."

"I really like you too."

Chapter Twenty-Three

It's eight in the morning and even though Catherine hasn't texted me back I'm dying to talk to her. After another agonizing ten minutes I decide to walk over there and knock. I know she has to be home. I walk quickly across the parking lot and around the small block of identical apartments until I reach Catherine and Nathan's little townhouse.

I have to knock on the door twice before Catherine answers. Her hair is sticking up in odd directions, and her shirt is hanging oddly from her shoulder. I don't think she's wearing pants. My heart twists as I'm reminded of the time that we lived together. Even though it was a hard year, I miss her. I miss having a companion. I hate having to admit how lonely I feel now. I spent so long ignoring the loneliness. I told myself it was better to be alone than deal with what might happen if I let people in. I was angry, and hurt, and trying to keep my battered heart as quiet as possible. Now that I've found my people who make me feel loved, the loneliness is harder to ignore and I find myself wanting more than I've had. I'm just so afraid to trust again and end up with someone who isn't giving me what I'm asking for.

Catherine shoos me inside with a yawn. "I just was about to text you back. Sorry, I got in late last night and Nathan kept me up later."

I smile at her because I really do love how much my friends love each other. Following her into the little kitchen that looks almost exactly like mine, I nudge her out of the way with my hip and reach for where I know they keep the coffee. Catherine wordlessly goes to sit at one of their bar stools and watches me drowsily.

"So, what's the major emergency?" She says around another yawn.

"I got almost naked with Saul, yesterday." Maybe the quieter I say it the less embarrassing it is.

There's a thunk and a grunt as I look over my shoulder as Catherine sits gaping at me. "You whaaat?" She grins so wide I have to look away as embarrassment overwhelms me.

"And then I freaked out and we didn't do anything else and I think he must think I'm an awful tease. I probably gave him the worst set of blue balls he's had since high school. I mean, I had every intention of doing something. We talked about sex, and he started throwing words out like protection and masturbation and somehow it was so hot. And I got so overwhelmed and then he was so comforting I thought it wouldn't be that hard to get naked with him. He feels so safe. But then he took my clothes off, and was saying such nice things about me, and kissing me and..." I drop my head into my hands as coffee starts to drip into the carafe. "And I just didn't know what to do. So I made him stop and I don't really think he understands. I don't know what to do but now he's seen my boobs and I don't know if I can ever make eye contact with him again."

Catherine furrows her eyebrows in contemplation. Making me absolutely want to die ten times more. She looks at me with the big hazel eyes and says "But did you get to see how big he was?"

I shriek, "WHAT?"

"Like you got kind of naked, so did he? Did you get to see anything? What's he look like without his clothes?" Catherine leans forward with a big grin like a high school girl looking for gossip.

"He's hot. Like surprisingly jacked in a runner kind of way. But uuuugh. I was not ready for it. His sweater vests do nothing for him." I lean back against the counter next to the coffee pot so that I'm facing her fully now. "And no, I wasn't paying attention to dick size. I was a bit distracted by everything else."

"That's the first thing I noticed about Nathan." Catherine winks at me and I want to hurl.

"Really? That's the first thing you noticed?" I lace my words with as much sarcasm as I can muster. "Nathan was just a walking penis? No arms or legs or massively broody personality? He didn't exist before his penis?"

"Nope, not with the way he wields it." She starts cackling so hard she starts tearing up. "You just forget anything from before it."

I sigh loudly and turn to pour us each a cup of coffee before walking around to sit next to her. I hear their bedroom door creak and see Nathan walks out in just a pair of PJ pants. He looks around confused and then makes eye contact with me as Catherine still is chuckling to herself.

"Hey, I heard laughing? What's so funny." Nathan cocks his head like a puppy.

"Apparently your penis." I say flatly.

"What!" Nathan's voice cracks. He looks to his feet with downcast eyes and a pouty lip. "My penis isn't that funny." He mutters.

"Listen, can we stop this." My face is on fire as Catherine laughs again with renewed mirth. "I don't want to know anything about your penis. To me you are a Ken doll down there. Is that better?"

"Not really." Nathan mutters under his breath as he walks to pour himself coffee.

"Your penis isn't funny." Catherine throws in with an eyebrow wiggle in my direction. "Now go take a shower."

"What? That's not fair. I never get to be a part of girl talk." Nathan pouts.

"Amber was in the middle of telling me about getting naked with Saul." Catherine says so matter of factly that I feel uncomfortable.

Nathan dumps hot coffee all over his hand and yelps. "Alright, shower here I come." He practically runs back down the hall toward the bathroom.

"Okay," Catherine takes a gulp of her coffee, "serious mode. So why are you freaking about this? You aren't dating, it's perfectly reasonable to not fuck before your official."

"I mean, like three weeks ago I couldn't stand him. Things feel like they've gone really fast, but I don't know. It's not just that. I feel like I don't know how to do this thing with him. I don't even know what this thing is. I mean, he's been extremely open and honest with me and it's freaking me out. What am I supposed to do with someone who says exactly what they want and feel?" I start chewing on my cheek anxiously.

"Praise the Lord for someone who's honest?" She raises her hands like she's in worship.

"It's more than that. He wants me to be the same way." I take another drink of coffee to stop myself from talking. The conversation is sounding more and more ridiculous to me as I talk.

"Do you hear yourself? Amber, you are upset someone wants more than a mediocre immature college relationship with you. You are freaking out because you can't just be some guy's arm candy. That's what it really is, someone has expectations for you to be in a relationship with you. When all you've ever had to be is the chick to take and claim at parties." Catherine's tone is trying to make it sound less harsh than the words she's saying are.

"Ouch. I mean, I know you're not wrong. You and Saul will get along great. I love being roasted before nine in the morning." I lean on the counter. "I do really like him. It just seems like so much. And he's actually so interesting and so willing to talk about things. I guess I'm really just worried that we're going to start to get to know each other, and what I have just isn't going to be enough."

"You might not be. I highly doubt it, but you two fit really well together. I also think if we get down to it you are focusing on this to avoid talking about what else is going on. I could see you and Saul getting married someday." She is far too nonchalant.

"I originally meant to come over here and tell you about coffee with my sister yesterday morning. And the letter she gave me. But then the naked thing happened and it just really threw me. Everything seems to be off right now. I don't know how to handle any of it well. For the record, marriage sounds terrifying. But I'll pin that for later to freak out about. I really don't know what to do about Brittany. Things have been so strained just knowing I could accidentally run into her around town. I barely want to leave my house at this point. When we talked yesterday, she said she would back off. I don't know if I believe her. I don't know if Andrew will keep his distance. And it just makes me sick. I lost everyone when they got together and moved away. I mean everyone. How am I supposed to just get over that now that she's here again. She gave me this letter yesterday that I read while I was at Saul's, and I honestly just don't know if it's enough. I don't know that I can just let things go because she finally said sorry. What they did broke something inside of me. Cheating sucks regardless, but cheating like that... behind my back for so long. With each other. And then they got to ride off into the sunset after bulldozing my life. My mom is still mad at me, and my dad doesn't come around anymore. I haven't had a normal birthday or holiday since. And they come back with a fucking baby that's basically a get-out-of-jail free card for all the shit they put me through because no one can be mad about a baby."

"I think you don't feel you've changed so they must not have. Sure you're definitely right Andrew hasn't. I can't say I really understand, but

I can say that even with my issues with my Dad I wish I hadn't missed so much of my sister's life. I barely knew Bailey, but now she calls me all the time. She's funny, smart, and cute. If you choose to fully cut off your sister then you fully cut off your niece or nephew. Nathan's nieces and nephews call me Aunt Cat, it's the coolest, and Nathan can barely stand Sofia. I can't decide for you and it's your life."

"To be fair, Sofia never fucked you behind Nathan's back and then told him it was his fault for being a boring prude."

Just then the bathroom door opens and Nathan comes down the hallway. "That was a visual I didn't need." Nathan sets his coffee cup in the sink and looks at me. "I don't mean to butt in, but Amber, I was there with you when everything went down, and I think your feelings are completely valid. But, people change. I never was a fan of Andrew. I think he can still shove it if I'm being honest. Brittany was basically a child then, though. You both were. Honestly she was barely an adult and it's creepy what Andrew did. Maybe you do owe it to yourself to know for sure before you shut that door. But also, if you want me to jump Andrew at any time. Just let me know."

I smile gratefully. "I know you guys are right. I think I just need more time to get a feel for things. Everything is happening so fast."

"I think it's fair to take time to decide." Catherine takes my hand reassuringly. "If your sister is asking you to be in her life, she will still be there a day or a month or even a year from now. And honestly that may be how you decide if she's changed. If she's serious about making an effort for the two of you to be close, she will wait until you decide to do something."

"I have to head into work, Amber, I'll see you later today?" Nathan is heading out of the kitchen and down the hall.

"Yeah, I'll be in."

"Excuuuuuse me." Catherine hops off her bar stool and tramps down the hall to the front door. "You forgot to kiss me." She huffs before I hear her giggle as I'm assuming Nathan does something sickeningly cute. When Catherine takes her seat again she is grinning to herself and her hair is even crazier than before.

"You're disgusting." I roll my eyes at her.

"You're just jealous you're not kissing Saul right now." She makes smoochie kisses at me. "Oh Saul my love will you marry meeee." Catherine's eyes become dreamy and she mocks me in a baby voice.

My heart sinks... Is Saul the guy I'm going to marry... I think I might puke.

Chapter Twenty-Four

Saul has called me three times today. I ignored them all. I mean two of the calls were at work. I think that's fair not to answer then. As if being at work ever has been a reason not to answer a call from Catherine. I'll talk to him at work tomorrow. It's not really a big deal, and it's not like he left a voicemail so it can't be that important.

When he called me at nine I was in the bath and probably could have answered but then I remembered him asking me about masturbation and wanted to die all over again. I spent the rest of my bath watching The Office reruns and hoping that when I let the water out I'd be swept away down the drain with it.

The following day at work he wasn't there either, and the day after that. I could have asked Nathan, and three times I thought about poking my head into his office to see what was going on. But every time I went to do it, I'd either talk myself out of it or get distracted. By Friday when we went for drinks at Cici's I was genuinely worried. That worry overshadowed the embarrassment of asking. But all Nathan could tell me was that Saul called in to use some of his vacation and he didn't give him an answer as to why.

"I don't understand why you didn't ask." I say, annoyed. "Or why didn't he tell you anything."

Nathan shrugged dismissively. "You know how Saul is, it's not like he thinks to say anything. He told me what I needed to know. I mean the phone call was like forty five seconds. I approved it and didn't have time to ask before he ended the call."

I huff in annoyance because I know Nathan is right. Saul wouldn't think details matter unless specifically asked.

By Tuesday of the next week I'm on the verge of calling him, staring at my phone. I don't know why it's taking me so long. I do, if I'm honest, but my favorite thing is to lie to myself so why stop now. Is that why he called? Is he dying? Did I scare him off?

OH MY GOD HE TOOK DAYS OFF TO AVOID ME!

My drive to the library fills my brain with dread. I can't believe I undressed, cock-teased him and then permanently traumatized him enough to take the week off work. I blast the radio and start sing screaming.

"Lonely, I'm Mr. Lonely

I have nobody for my own

Now I am so lonely, I'm Mr. Lonely

Wish I had someone to call on the phone."

I pull into my spot and use a little powder to hide my puffy eyes from crying. I step out of the car and look up and see his truck.

"Oh fuck..." I say to myself. Breathe, it's fine Amber. It's a huge library, I can definitely avoid him until I'm ready. I know, I'll walk in and start straight on putting books away. I stumble a little as I climb the stairs to the library. Then I can have time to formulate what to say. Then I can grab a book that I need to show him and that can be the lead off to our conversation.

"Oh no..." I whisper as I swing open the door. Saul is at the front desk... Saul is waving at me. Kill me now.

My hand rises on its own to wave back as dread fills me. "Hey." I squeak out as I round the desk. Before I can put my things down Saul's arm is around my waist and his lips brush against my cheek and my heart stops. I freeze. I don't pull away, I don't lean in, I don't even think I blink. I'm just frozen. My brain is blissfully terrifyingly empty as Saul pulls back to study my face.

"Why do you look like you shit your pants?" He says finally.

"Because I am about to." I blurt out. "You hated me so much you took a whole week off work!"

"What?" He cocks his head to the side.

"I gave you the worst case of blue balls, destroyed your ego, then ghosted you, so you left." A tear runs down my cheek.

"You ghosted me?" Saul's eyebrows furrowed in confusion.

"Isn't that why you weren't at work all last week? I ruined this thing between us." I'm trying to calm myself down, because the genuine confusion in Saul's eyes is starting to make me feel crazy.

"No?" Saul lets go of me and takes a step back. I feel the distance like a cold bucket of water. "My mom had an eye infection. My brother needed help taking care of her. I went and stayed with them for the week so he didn't have to worry about her. I'm much better with schedules and keeping on top of her meds than he is." He sits down in my chair. "You thought what happened, now?"

"That I gave you such a severe case of blue balls you had to take off work to avoid me." As I say it out loud I want to jump off a cliff.

"Oh it's not a big deal. I just masturbated after you left. This wouldn't be the first issue with 'blue balls' I've ever had." He shrugs.

"Well, then, I'm... I'm gonna go stack books... bye.." I say stuttering.

"Okay have fun." He goes back to doing what he was before.

I start to walk away, "Wait." I whip back around. "You're not bothered? At all?"

"No?" He looks up quizzically.

"Well, okay, fine." I feel a rush of annoyance. He was gone a whole week after I embarrassed myself and didn't say anything? "Whatever." I grab the cart off returned books aggressively and stomp roll away. He tried to call three times, that's it! I was in a panic, I mortified myself the day before and he barely tried to check on me.

I feel myself start to angrily shoving books on the shelves. He didn't even care. I have been losing my shit all week at work, thinking that something was actually wrong and it was basically nothing. At least nothing that had to do with us. Why didn't he at least send a text, or check in again? Maybe I should just let it go. Maybe this whole thing isn't nearly as important to him as it is to me. I know he said that he liked me, but maybe after everything he did realize that it wasn't going to be worth it. Or maybe he just wants things to be more casual than we originally thought and he just didn't say anything to me about it.

"Hey..." I jump as Saul suddenly materializes beside me.

I place a hand on my chest to settle my racing heart. "Saul, hey." I straighten and grab another book, trying to look like I wasn't just spiraling in the fiction section. "You should really walk louder or something, you scared me shitless."

"I walked like I always do, you were just so busy abusing those poor books..." I think he is trying to be funny but I just side-eye him and keep going. After a moment he clears his throat and continues to talk, "I was attempting to look at the schedule for study rooms downstairs and couldn't focus because I feel like I've done something wrong and I don't know what I did." He looks sheepish from the corner of my eye and I feel bad so I turn to give him my attention.

"I don't know." I sigh. "Do you even like me? Because you were gone a whole week and left me sitting paranoid. You only called like three times on the day after. Then never again." I feel sick to my stomach.

"I mean, I called three times and you didn't answer. I didn't think it was that big of a deal. I try not to call anyone more than three times. I have a rule. Otherwise I'd call you a hundred times in an hour."

"Oh... I am not sure how to be angry with you." I shake my head. "Cause that makes sense. But I still feel... I don't know."

"I'm not sure I have an answer for you. I don't really know how to communicate with you if when I try to, you don't answer the phone. Maybe I should have sent a text, but ignoring three calls kind of feels like you don't want to talk. Or you're busy. I mean, I don't owe you anything, really." He smiles at me like that takes the harshness out of what he's saying.

"I want you to though. Not like being indebted forever to me or something. I guess I want to be important to you. I didn't want to talk, but I wanted you to push. I guess I haven't told you to. You're right you aren't obligated to me but... I want you to... I want more than I think we have established."

"I didn't know. I'm glad you told me. I'm not completely sure that I understand what you mean, but I can try harder to communicate. I really like you. But, if you want more from me, I think you are going to have to give me more in return. I can't be the only one making an effort. You can't ignore my calls in the future and then get mad that I didn't try hard enough to contact you. And you can't keep your feelings bottled up because I don't know. I won't know." He sighs frustrated, but not with me, I think with himself. "If I could just pick up on that stuff I promise you I would... But I just can't and being with me means you have to be okay with that."

"You're right I know you are." I look down at my nervous feet tapping and twisting about. "I feel so immature and childish. I want... I want to be yours and I want you to be mine. I'm insecure, I have no certainty in what we have right now. We almost had sex the other day and I just felt like you only wanted me for that. I've never slept with anyone I wasn't in a relationship with. I am not a fuck buddy kind of chick. I'm afraid that's where this is going." My stomach lurches, I realize that's why I'm actually upset. It's not being ignored, Andrew did plenty of that. It's the uncertainty in what we are and what we're going to be.

"I'm really glad you said something. I didn't know. If a label makes this easier, I'm all for it. Labeling and organizing things is where I accel." He wiggles his eyebrows at me to lighten the mood. "Amber, will you be my girlfriend?" He pauses, thinks and chuckles "Should I like, get down on one knee or something?"

I laugh a little, feeling the tension ease between us. "Please don't. But I'd like that a lot, you can save the whole 'getting down on one knee' thing for when you ask me to marry you someday..." Panic crosses across my face and his. "I'M SO SORRY FRUIDEN SLIP!" I take a deep breath. "Well I guess saying dumb things when I'm anxious is what you have to be okay with."

Saul steps forward hesitantly and wraps his arms around me, sobering a little. "And I meant what I said last week. If you're not ready for more, I'm not pushing for more. We can be in a relationship and go as slowly as you need to. But I'm here when you're ready. I'll follow your lead in all of this." He brushes his nose and lips across my cheek in the sweetest gesture. "Whatever you want, I just want you."

My heart is in my throat and I work to swallow around it as I let him hold me and the tension of the last week and all of my confused feelings melt away. I wrap my arms around his neck and we just stand there for longer than is probably appropriate at work. I'm thankful no one walks down the aisle or bothers us.

His deep brown eyes pull me in. His smile turns in one corner, making my heart skip a beat. He looks at my lips with a hunger that tells me it's taking all his will power not to kiss me. I have less self control and stand on my tip toes to go in for a kiss. Our lips connect and it's like fireworks. Tingles run down my spine. His lips are so soft I could melt into them. When I pull away his eyes are glazed and his smile grows from ear to ear.

"Uhm, I was going to go back to the desk but I need a minute..." Sauls cheeks turn bright red.

"Why do..." Then I feel him against my stomach. I softly push him away. "How about I stock these shelves and you... you go stand over there."

"Ha..ha.. Yeah." Saul pecks me on the head and goes a few feet away and faces the bookshelf far too close to it.

Chapter Twenty-Five

"So why have you called us both in here?" I ask Nathan, annoyance thick in my voice. My shift ended twenty minutes ago. I need to get home to change for our double date. Saul is sitting in the chair next to me twiddling his thumbs and looking around the room.

"I sort of feel like I'm in detention." Saul mutters.

"Well, we need to talk about Library policy. I was notified by security that you two were... uhm *canoodling* in the aisles." Nathan sighs "So as your relationship continues, that can't be on the premises."

Saul speaks. "Did you mean coitus? Because we definitely weren't doing that. We just made out a few times."

I mentally facepalm hard enough to roll my eyes. "Saul, that's what he's talking about."

Nathan's face reddens. "Yes, all of that. I don't want security getting an eyeful when they check the cameras in the evenings."

"They wouldn't. Nothing's happened like that, Nathan." I say indignantly. "And don't even start with me, I know what you've done in this office."

Nathan's face turns a deep shade of scarlet. "Amber, you know what I mean."

"I don't." Saul pipes up.

"So, as long as there are no cameras, it's fine?" I ask, giving him a knowing look.

"I…" Nathan stutters and pauses to collect his thoughts. "How about we just leave it at that."

"Alright, so next time no cameras. Got it." I stand to leave, motioning for Saul to do the same. He's still staring between us like he's missing something and I nod toward the door with my head hoping he gets the memo that I'll tell him outside. "See you tonight Nathan!" I call over my shoulder, pulling the door closed behind me.

"I don't get it." Saul says when we're alone. "What happened in his office?"

I grin at him and wiggle my eyebrows. When he still stares at me blankly, I sigh. "When he and Catherine first started dating, they had a bad habit of having their hands down each other's pants in his office during the work day."

Saul's eyes go wide in understanding. "Oh, so that's why he wouldn't open the door that one time and just yelped at me to go away."

"Yeeep. It's disgusting. I'm afraid to touch anything in that room." I kiss Saul quickly while we wait for the elevator. "I'll see you later, right? For drinks after work? I'm going to go home and get ready."

"Of course, I'll meet you there?"

It's right after nine when I see Saul walk into Cici's bar. I want to roll my eyes because he came in work attire. His buttoned up look has started to grow on me the last few weeks, and at least he's started wearing his nose ring even to work. But the straight poop brown sweater vest he's sporting over the light blue button down doesn't do anything for him. The combination sweater vest, nose ring, coke bottle glasses, and slicked back hair is the weirdest thing. And I hate that it turns me on a little.

Saul gives a little wave as he approaches, and Nathan gives him one of those weird hand shake hugs men do.

We've already ordered drinks, and I got Saul a tea just like he got before. He sits beside me, and puts his arm around my shoulder, kissing my cheek. I smile up at him but the little bubble that formed as soon as he touched me pops when I hear Catherine make a gagging sound.

Without even looking at her I say, "Can it Catherine, I've had to put up with you and Nathan for far too long."

Nathan snorts into his diet coke and Catherine giggles. I take the chance to press my lips quickly to Saul's before turning back to the table, leaning into Saul's side. "So, Catherine, did Nathan tell you he actually told us we weren't allowed to make out in the library today?"

Catherine turns her attention to Nathan, as he looks like he might spontaneously combust. "No, he didn't."

"I just meant they can't be making out on camera." Nathan says defensively.

"I seem to remember a super inappropriate make out session in the aisles when I worked there. A few, actually. It was crazy, my boss totally kept coming onto me." Catherine side-eyes me and winks.

"I AM THE BOSS I LEGALLY HAVE TO SAY SOMETHING!" Nathan whines.

"Sure, sounds like you're a creep watching footage of people making out." I egg him on more.

"I am NOT. I didn't even watch I got second hand informed by the fucking security guys." He plants his face firmly in his palms.

Catherine and I burst into laughter as Nathan tries to defend himself. Then Nathan goes dead silent and elbows Catherine. He whispers in her ear and she goes silent too. Saul is swirling his tea with his straw and doesn't notice the awkward looks on their faces.

"Uh. Secrets, secrets are no fun. Secrets, secrets hurt someone." I state indignantly.

They both give each other looks and Nathan nods pointing his chin behind me. I turn and there stands Andrew at the bar glaring with full force at our table. I whip my head around in a panic and grab Saul's thigh. He finally looks up from his tea.

"Huh?" He grunts.

"Andrew's here..." I say gritting my teeth. "And he's staring down our table like a fucking psycho."

"Which one?" Saul turns around in the most obvious way to look.

"Oh the big black guy who is staring down the table?"

"Stop it shhh." I smack his leg. "I would rather pretend he's not here."

"Well I don't think that's gonna happen." Nathan says nervously.

"Why?" I ask completely clueless.

"Cause he's walking straight towards us." Catherine says her brows furrowed like she is about to launch into a fight.

"Oh fuck…" I feel myself shrink in my seat.

"Hey, you and I need to talk." Andrew slurs out from behind me. Of course, he's drunk.

"I don't think you do." Saul interjects.

"Who the fuck are you?" Andrew hisses.

I sigh loudly and dramatically. "What do you want?"

"You haven't responded to MY wife's letter. It's been a week and she's fucking devastated." Andrew clenches his fists.

"I remember distinctly telling MY sister that I would think about it, IF you two left me alone." I say snidely and turn back to my drink and take a sip. "Speaking of, where is she?"

"Out with your mom." I don't bother to look at him. I know his lips are snarled and angry. He makes the ugliest angry faces.

"Good for her." I keep my eyes on my drink even though jealousy is coursing through me hot and destructive. I haven't seen or spent time with my mother in years. Obligatory angry Christmas dinners aside, I honestly can't remember the last time I 'went out with my mom'. I squash the dizzying longing and attempt to make it look like I'm finished with the conversation.

"I really don't understand why this feud is still so heavy between all of us. I mean, grow the fuck up Amber, move on. Why can't we just get past this shit. It's exhausting." Andrew says nonchalantly, but he's swaying dangerously on his feet.

"Well, until you do understand, I have no interest in 'moving on'. Thanks, have a great day." My tone is heavy with sarcasm.

"God, you are sucha stuck up cunt..." He slurs out.

Saul is on his feet and standing in front of Andrew before anyone can register what's happening. Everything slows down around us as I take in my scrawny nerdy boyfriend ready to defend my honor against a man who stands almost a full head above him.

"Hey, you cannot say that." Saul interjects.

"What are you gonna do about it, you twiggy bitch?" Andrew smirks and gets that look on his face. The same look he'd give in bars when we were dating to get the other guy to swing first.

"Andrew, you're drunk. You need to go." I say also getting to my feet. But I can't hold back all of the nasty comments flying through my head, and they tumble out of my mouth before I can catch them. "I mean, look at you. Still trying to start drunken fights like in college. Some dad you'll be. You know, I thought after watching your dad spend his nights drunk off his ass, you'd learn, but I guess the apple doesn't fall far from the tree." The words feel like poison dripping from my mouth. This isn't me but Andrew can always draw this person out.

Andrew takes a menacing step forward, but he's cut off by Saul.

"Amber, what are you even saying right now?" Saul says, looking at me like I grew a third eye. "I think you both need to go your separate ways." He says, looking at me pointedly. But I can see over his shoulder where Andrew looks like his head is about to explode.

"This is between her and I." Andrew shoves Saul to the side. "You're just fucking pissed we got a happily fucking forever while you sit bitter and fucking stuck. What have you even fucking done with your life? We don't fucking need you in our life, I don't fucking even want you in it. We're all waaay better off without you bitchy stuck up fucking attitude. Brittany fuckin wants you. She thinks you deserve to be an aunt. But I know what this is really about, your pissed that the prettier sister won and always fucking will."

Nathan stands to his feet and Catherine runs off. "Alright, enough is enough." He rolls up his sleeves. "I'm going to give you about ten seconds to tuck your tail and run. As a courtesy to your father." Nathan links his fingers cracking his knuckles.

"What are you gonna fuckin do, beaner." Suddenly, Andrew drops in the process of Nathan lunging over the table.

"I don't owe your dad a damn thing, dude." Larry stands, shaking out his only hand, staring icily down at Andrew who looks like he's seeing stars on the ceiling of the bar. Did Larry really just punch Andrew in the back of the head?!

Catherine is standing back a few steps with her hands over her mouth, horror etched into every part of her face. I feel like I can't hear anything over the waterfall roaring through my ears as my pulse pounds behind my eyes like I'm the one that just got hit.

Everyone in the bar is staring at us, it's gone eerily quiet as people openly watch this horror show like it's a b-rated scary movie showing on Halloween. The actors are paid shit, and everything seems cheesy and more dramatic than it needs to be. But I guess this is my life. Again. Flashes of that awful night years ago spring up in my memory. It was another night that Andrew and I got into a fight about my sister. But last time she opened his door in an oversized tshirt and sex hair. Last time we were alone in the night when awful words spewed between us like fire. And it was me who hit him. Last time, it was only me who got hurt. This time my drama touches everyone I care about. This time everyone suffers for something that maybe I should just be able to get over. Maybe Andrew is right and it's better if I just bow out with grace. If I have any grace or dignity left after tonight. It feels like I was caught with my skirt tucked into my underwear as sheer mortification lances through me like a hot poker to the gut. I want to double over, put my hands on my knees and breathe, but I can't manage to do anything but stare blankly at the chaos around me.

There's hands on my shoulders, and Saul's face comes into view as he looks me over like he's looking for injuries. When his eyes meet mine I have no idea what he sees, but he's leaning over, picking up my unicorn purse from the booth, throwing it over his shoulder. If I wasn't sure I was about to die of a panic attack I'd probably laugh at how much more stupid the lavender and pink bag makes his outfit look. Saul is saying something to Nathan, but my eyes are glued to where Charlie and Larry are hoisting Andrew off the dirty barroom floor. Andrew finally looks quelled, staring at his shoes and refusing to look anyone in the eye.

Nathan comes into view as he steps closer to me. After he looks at me, he must know that I'm incapable of communication right now. So he just gives me a grim look and turns to find Catherine where she is talking animatedly into her phone.

Saul is back in front of me, cupping my face so softly between his hands. His thumbs brush my wet cheeks, wiping away tears I couldn't feel. "Let's go." He says, but his voice sounds like he's under water. His warm arm comes around my shoulders as he steers my numb body out of the door and ushers me into his truck. He opens the passenger door, leaning over me to put my bag on the seat. I get a whiff of his clean scent and it's like all of my senses come back into sharp focus all at once.

I gasp, clutching at my throat like I can rip off whatever thing is suffocating me slowly.

"Can I take you home with me?" Saul asks, quietly.

I nod because I still can't speak. My half-finished cocktail feels like bile in my stomach, threatening to come back up my throat. I close my eyes and focus on my breathing, trying to get my emotions under control. I feel heavy like my body is a sack of potatoes. I feel my eyes flutter as the sudden rush of adrenaline drops. I lay my head against the cold window and fall asleep.

Chapter Twenty-Six

"Hey, we're here." Saul nudges me awake. I nod and roll myself out of his truck. He walks around and puts his arm around me. "I'm always a little shaky after a panic attack, here, let me help you balance."

He helps me up his front steps and through the door. The purple lights are far more mysterious at night. A small white humidifier hisses at the corner of his living room. I walk to the giant beanbag surrounded by tropical plants and fall into it. I throw my hands over my face and let out a muffled "This is absolute bullshit."

"Do you want to talk about it?" Sauls voice is hesitant.

"No... Yes... I am literally ruining everyone around me's life. I'm not only fucking my sister over but now the three most important people to me lives. LARRY IS GONNA GO TO JAIL AND IT'S ALL MY FAULT!" I feel the tears start welling in my eyes.

"Why exactly is Larry going to jail?" Saul settles himself in the beanbag next to me and wraps me in his arms. We sink awkwardly into the overstuffed fuzzy seat, and it feels like our bodies meld together every-where we touch.

"He assaulted Andrew." I say burying my face in his shoulder, holding back tears.

"I'm pretty sure Andrew was the one who started everything, if anything, Andrew should go to jail for disorderly conduct. He would have attacked one or all of us if Larry hadn't stepped in. Plus I think he's technically the bouncer so he can take care of unruly customers."

"I guess. But it shouldn't have happened to begin with. I don't know what to do. I mean, they're home for a few weeks, and nothing has changed. And it's total shit, he brings out the absolute worst in me. I mean, I said stupid shit and pissed him off even more. Why did I do that? It was so stupid."

"Yeah, it kind of was stupid." Saul states. Something snaps in me.

"Excuse me?" I hiss.

"You egged him on instead of dropping it. It is at least a little on you." Saul says it so matter of factly as if he has no idea he is cutting me so deep.

"He fucking used me, he was a ass and then fucked my little sister." I sit up. "He was my everything and threw it away. I responded to him like that because he's always this way."

"I understand that, but you're acting like this was months ago, not years ago. Even if he hasn't changed, you're fighting like you want to hurt him, like he still means something to you. I don't get it." Saul is still holding me, but right now I want to rip myself out of his arms. "I mean, it's like you still have feelings for him."

I snap. I squirm awkwardly out of the beanbag to look down at him, "I mean, of course I still have feelings. I have feelings because he was supposed to be my first and last. He was supposed to be everything and protect me, and instead he broke me. Not like you'd understand, you act like a robot half the time," Anger boils over, "I want a fucking love story and you are sooo fucking chill nothing bothers you. At least I'm fucking passionate, if we break up you'd probably wouldn't even fucking notice."

Saul's eyes for a split second convey so much hurt it makes me want to physically vomit. Then they go flat and unfeeling. He pushes himself from the beanbag, adjusts his shirt and walks past me. "I think you should go." he says flat, cold and heartlessly.

"Fine, I WILL!" I snap, not willing to back down.

I storm past him and slam his front door. It echoes loudly through the quiet night. The cold air sends a shiver up my spine. I angrily stomp down the steps and realize I have no way to get home. It's a ten minute drive to my apartment but nearly an hour walk and I'm in heels. I hit the call button and wait for Catherine to pick up. Nothing but dial tone. I pop off my heels and put them in my unicorn backpack and start walking.

"Wait, do you need me to drive you home." Saul shouts from his porch.

"NO!" I angrily shout back.

I hear a door shut. I'm on my own. Stuck alone with my own thoughts. I really am on a roll of ruining people's lives. God, I can't believe I called him a robot. Did we just break up? I mean neither of us said anything. Couples fight all the time. But they also don't attack each other's character. God and I essentially almost made Nathan fight my ex. Catherine looked terrified. I've had absolute peace for years. Everything was steady and predictable.

Now I have no idea what's going to happen tomorrow, let alone the next five minutes. A car zooms past me honking at me. If I get hit by a car right now I wouldn't be too upset about it. I am gonna have to quit my job at the library if Saul and I broke up just now. This is why I need to stop putting myself out there. All I do is hurt people. I put Saul in such a shitty position and then insulted him.

My phone starts vibrating about forty minutes into my walk. I pull it out of my pocket and a smiling Catherine is flashing from it. I want to answer but I suddenly want to ignore it. I fight off that bitter feeling and pick up.

"Hey..." I answer as my voice cracks.

"What's going on? I thought you were with Saul."

"I fucked everything up Catherine." Here comes the tears. "I'll be there in like twenty minutes."

"Do you need us to pick you up?" Her voice sounds like she just finished a jog. Oh no... *Gross.*

"NO!" I shout, "I'll walk, I'm almost there anyway." I sigh.

"Okay good that gives me time to shower. I'll see you in twenty." Click.

"Yeah see you in twenty." I say as I put my phone back in my pocket.

I knock on the door at least four times. I can hear footsteps approach the door, they're heavy so it must be Nathan. The door swings open and there stands Nathan. He's in a pair of blue flannel pj's with a ratty old BGC shirt on. He looks me up and down and steps aside for me to come through without a word. I go and replace his spot on the couch and fall into Catherines lap groaning.

"Seriously? At least let me have the couch." Nathan groans.

"No." Catherine and I say in unison.

"Fine... But I'm taking the popcorn." He snatches the bowl from the coffee table and pouts all the way to their room.

"Someday I'll have my shit together." I say into the living room. "And I won't ruin all of your guys' date nights."

Catherine huffs out a laugh that doesn't quite sound believable. "You remember how many nights I fell apart in the beginning. Don't worry about it, what are friends for if not this?"

"I guess." I sit up and grab a pillow, wrapping my arms around it and holding it to my chest. "I'm sorry I ruined your night. Here and earlier at the bar."

"You didn't ruin our night. Andrew ruined our night." Catherine says seriously. "Don't blame yourself, that's not fair. You aren't responsible for anyone's choices but your own."

I groan and shove my face into the pillow as tears burn behind my eyes. "But then I egged Andrew on, and Saul and I got into a huge fight. I said so many stupid things tonight I just want to die."

"Why did you guys fight?"

"He told me I shouldn't have egged Andrew on. And he's right. But then he started acting like I still had feelings for Andrew and I don't know what happened. I snapped. I called him a robot and he asked me to leave. I don't know if we broke up, I mean we're barely together and I'm the biggest dick around because I know Saul isn't a robot, he's just so honest, and so matter of fact, and sometimes I just feel like he doesn't understand anything that's going on and I just need him to get things so that I don't always have to explain myself." I take a few sobbing breaths and sniff loudly. "And I'm a massive dick because he can't always help it, and I know that and I get mad anyway."

"Okay, yes you shouldn't have egged him on. I have been face to face with my dick of an ex and it's nearly impossible to hold back. In a way you do have feelings. I still think about Marcus. Saul should be more under-standing, men are dense but not that dense that he can't pick up on that. He can help understand that he is not that socially inept." She says while brushing my hair back.

"He kind of is though. I don't know who knows, but Saul told me at the very beginning of us talking that he's autistic. So he kind of struggles in high emotion situations. And I try my best to be patient, it's just hard sometimes because I want him to get it without me having to explain myself. But I can't always do that. It's so weird, because sometimes I feel like he does know. Like when I was losing it a few weeks ago, or when we almost got naked together in his room. It was like he got everything and even understood things that I wasn't sure I understood about how I was feeling. But then tonight he just kept pushing and asking questions and making comments that felt like shit, It was like he couldn't stop himself and I didn't know what to do."

"Pause that thought… NATHAN!" Catherine shouts so loud my ears start ringing again. I hear clambering from the bedroom.

"WHAT? IS EVERYTHING OKAY?" He comes out, almost out of breath.

"Did you know Saul was autistic?" Catherine asks, like a trick question.

"Yes…?" Nathan looks so confused.

"So for as long as I've known Saul, you've allowed me TO MOCK HIS SOCIAL INEPTNESS." She slides off her slipper and tosses it at him.

Nathan dodges the slipper expertly like he's used to it. "I didn't know if I could say anything. It's not like a big deal, he's fine, he just doesn't get social stuff and is weird about corduroy." Nathan shrugs.

"Seriously, though, I have been being shitty, and you said nothing." Catherine glares.

"Maybe just stop being shitty?" Nathan says, teasingly.

"No, I say what I want." She sticks out her tongue. "Wait, what do you mean about corduroy?"

"Don't even get me started on that. I am not reliving that moment." He says.

"Fine, I'll ask him next week." Catherine states.

"What if we're broken up?" I want to sob.

"Did he say you're over?" Nathan asks.

"No... But..." I must have ruined it. It was totally a break up fight.

"Then you're not. Saul is matter of fact. You probably hurt his feelings, but Saul's clear cut. He would have told you if you were broken up before speaking another word. Saul's probably at home rocking with his noise canceling headphones on and googling 'how to fix your girlfriend'." Nathan sighs, "Saul is the kindest guy ever, but he is blunt and honest– sometimes to a fault. If you can't do that then you shouldn't be with him. I don't necessarily think that's his autism, that's just who he is. He doesn't get social cues but he's one of the wisest men I've ever met. You two go well together and you know deep down you appreciate his honesty. You're just used to people using honesty as a weapon." Nathan tosses a handful of popcorn in his mouth.

"Nice, that was really good." Catherine says smiling. "You're so hot when you say the smart stuff."

Nathan winks at her. "I try, and it's all true. It's a new relationship you both are working out the kinks. He knows that. Your anxiety just rules your decision making." Nathan shrugs. "You really need a therapist."

"I am so annoyed at how right you are. Thank you." I let out a soft chuckle.

"Thank my therapist." He turns and shuts himself back into their room.

"Will you take me back to Saul's?" I ask. "I need to apologize..."

Chapter Twenty-Seven

"Are you sure you don't want me to wait here for a few minutes?" Catherine is holding my hand across the console while I bolster the courage I need to go back to the door.

I shake my head, "no." I don't think I'll be going home tonight, but if I do, then I will probably want to walk home like a pathetic loser wallowing in all of my self pity and missed opportunities.

"Alright," she gives my hand a squeeze. "Well, call me if you need me. And if you don't at least text me by noon tomorrow I will come looking for you."

"Thanks, love you." I hope she knows I mean that.

"Love you too." I close the car door behind me and watch until her tail lights disappear at the end of the street.

I hope Saul is still awake. It's ten minutes until midnight and I didn't really think this through before just showing back up. What if he does have noise canceling headphones on and can't hear me banging on the door?

There are a million variables and a million ways that the next ten minutes can go. I mentally hike up my big girl panties and get ready to face the music. I know I've messed up a lot with Saul, and I feel like I can't promise for things to be better. But I care enough about him that I need to try. No matter what, he's completely changed the trajectory of my life. I just hope he cares enough about me and our relationship to give me another chance. And another chance after that because I'm sure I will mess up again.

My knuckles hit the door all of one time before Saul yanks it open and I almost hit him in the chest.

"Oh, thank God." Saul takes one step onto the porch and wraps his arms around me so tightly it knocks the breath right out of me. I'm so shocked I don't even know how to respond. The arm I used to knock is still awkwardly off to the side slowly falling out of the air and the other is thrown out for balance. "I was going to give you until morning before I came and found you but I was hoping that you would come back." Saul holds me back at arms length taking in my surprised and confused expression. I don't know what he sees, but his face falls into confusion as well. "Are you here to break up with me?" He looks hesitant and removes his hands from me. I feel the instant coldness where his hands were and want it back.

"No, I was coming back to beg you not to break up with me." I say.

Saul's expression is unreadable as he takes my hand. "Let's go inside."

My heart is thundering in my chest as he leads the way, stopping to lock the door before we head toward the kitchen. The purple grow lights make me feel like I'm in a sci-fi movie. Saul looks like he was in the middle of a massive manic reorganization frenzy and I wonder if he cleans and moves stuff when he's anxious. Unlike me, I let things pile up when I get overwhelmed.

"What were you doing?" I ask, looking around.

"Packing orders, I couldn't sit still."

There's a pair of black, noise canceling headphones sitting on the counter, and I point to them. "What are those for?"

Saul walks over to them and picks them up, holding them out to me. "Sometimes, when I'm overstimulated or overwhelmed it becomes harder to block out the noise around me. The grow lights can make a pretty intense buzzing noise and sometimes I can't handle it. Or the sound of the humidifier, fridge, and any other electricity or outside noises. It helps me center myself and think."

I take them, studying them. "They look like the headphones that my dad uses at the shooting range."

"They're similar. These are bluetooth though and I can turn on an extra level of noise canceling. They have tiny little microphones here–" He points to little holes on the sides of the earcups. "When I turn them on, they listen for the sounds around me and emit opposite frequencies to cancel out the noise. You can try them on, if you push the button on the left ear cup they turn on."

Saul watches me closely as I put them on and push the button. Silence like I haven't experienced before floods my senses. It feels tactile, like a weighted blanket settling over my system. I can hear my heartbeat and the sound of my breathing, but even that feels muffled under the silence. Without thinking I close my eyes and it's like the world around me disappears. I didn't know a house could be so noisy until the sound was taken away. I count to ten in my head, surprised by how much I enjoy the sensory deprivation. When I open my eyes again Saul is wearing a knowing look, like he understands what I'm thinking and feeling.

I turn the headphones off and take them off, looking at them in my hands instead of looking at Saul. "I'm really sorry I'm the reason the world got so loud." I say quietly.

Saul doesn't say anything for a long moment, but takes the headphones out of my hands and places them on the counter. "It's okay." He says, cupping my face, forcing me to look at him. "It's quieter now." His eyes hold so much affection and compassion I feel my heart press painfully against my ribs like it's suddenly grown too big for its place inside my chest.

"I'm sorry I asked you to leave earlier." He says without letting go of me. "It was the wrong thing to do."

"No, I think it was the right thing to do. I was being an ass." My throat feels like it could close up at any second.

"You were a little." He admits and I try not to let his words sting. "But I should have been more understanding of the situation. I called my mom after you left, and told her what was going on and she ripped me a new one, telling me I was a total dick. It wasn't my place to correct you, that wasn't very 'supportive boyfriend' of me. I know you don't still have feelings like that for Andrew, and I know that him and Brittany being here again is stirring up a lot of bad shit. He was the asshole in the situation tonight. He's been the asshole in the situation the whole time. I feel like sometimes I just have trouble putting myself in other people's places when things happen. I don't mean to be so clinical. Sometimes I feel like it helps me understand, and other times it just falls flat." His voice cracks a little, that the same fear is bubbling up in him.

"You called your mom?" I ask incredulously. I'm not upset as much as I am surprised. I couldn't imagine being able to call one of my parents, especially my mom after something high stress like this to talk through a situation.

"Yeah, I'm sorry if that was the wrong thing to do—telling her what was going on—it's just that sometimes she really helps me see if I was the problem in a situation." He leans against the counter opposite me and crosses his arms. "She and I have gotten really close over the years. She's an extremely amazing person, I want you to meet her sometime."

"I'd really like that." I sigh. "I do have to say something though, before we go further."

Saul doesn't say anything but inclines his head like he's listening. His face is open like he's ready for whatever it is without judgment. I had some time to think on the walk to Catherine and Nathan's and one part of tonight has been nagging at me since I cooled down.

"While I appreciate you stepping in when Andrew was being unreasonable, I need you not to tell me if I'm being crazy in front of people. It kind of defeats the purpose of me standing up for myself. Even if I'm doing it wrong. I need to be able to do it wrong on my own. You know?"

Saul is extremely quiet and still for a few minutes while he thinks and I struggle not to squirm in front of him while I wait.

"My mom has this saying that she reminded me of tonight. 'Support in public, correct in private. I struggle to not say what I'm thinking. I understand that was wrong, it seems we both have areas to work on to make this relationship work. But I refuse not to stand up for you. You asked me to help you feel wanted. Ignoring you getting berated would be the exact opposite of that. Nathan was about to fight Andrew and I'm certain you didn't say anything to him." My heart drops. He's right, I said nothing to Nathan but here I am complaining that my boyfriend defended me. "I won't promise not to fight for you because you deserve people in your life that are willing to do it. I'm not only willing but I want to. I have a black belt you know, and I'm not going to listen to anyone belittle and berate and name call the person I love. I felt downright murderous when Andrew spewed all of that vile ignorant hate toward you. I'm not going to apologize for getting between you two, but I will apologize for what I said. If our relationship is going to work, you have to let me be there for you like you are for me."

"Did you say the person you love?" A smile grows across my face while Saul's turns bright red.

"I guess I did..." His lips curl into a bashful side smile. "I love you

Amber... I've never had anyone like you in my life. When I said I was autistic you didn't suddenly look at me like I'm beneath you. That I'm a charity project." He reaches and holds my hands. " I know your thoughts swallow you whole sometimes and mine spill out of me uncontrollably. We're not perfect, and the best thing is from the start you haven't tried to be. I don't want to ruin what we have. You are the most authentic person I've ever met. I love your blonde hair and your blue eyes, they are almost as bright as your personality. I could stand in the rays of your joy forever. Even before you realized I was more than a nuisance." He puts his hand to my cheek and runs his thumb across my lips. "Your lips are so soft and scarlet like the wings of a cinnabar butterfly. I want to spend all day kissing them." He lifts my chin and kisses me. If this was a rom-com the camera would spin around us as fireworks go off in the background.

"I love you too." I say as I pull away.

"Thank God otherwise that whole speech would've been horribly awkward." We both laugh. He pulls me in and holds me tight. I nuzzle into his warmth and sigh a breath of relief.

Chapter Twenty-Eight

"Do you want me to drive you home?" Saul whispers gently into my hair.

"I want to stay in your arms forever." I grumble into his pecs.

"You could stay the night..." His heart picks up pace. "We don;t have to share a bed... I have an air mattress and..."

"I just said I want to stay in your arms forever." I meet his dark brown eyes with my own.

"I just..." I put a finger over his stuttering lips.

"Oh, toucha, toucha, toucha, TOUCH ME, I wanna be dirty, Thrill me, chill me, fulfill me, creature of the night." I say as I pull him towards the door that leads upstairs to his bedroom.

"Are you sure?" He asks hesitantly. "Wait, you've seen Rocky Horror Picture Show but not Little Shop of Horrors?"

"Only thing I've been sure of in years... Now stop fighting before my anxiety convinces me out of it." My voice drips with want and need. "And EVERYONE has seen Rocky Horror. If you didn't go through a phase where Tim Curry briefly made you question your sexuality, then I don't know if we can be friends."

"Okay." Saul scoops me up.

I feel as light as a feather in his arms. He carries me up the stairs and through his bug room. He sits down on the edge of the bed and maneuvers me to straddle him. I wrap my arms around his neck. I kiss him as I rock on his hips. I wait for the fear and anxiety to consume me, but it doesn't come. He runs his hands up my bare thighs, stopping once they reach my hips under my dress. I feel bolder without trepidation muddling my thoughts, and I take a handful of his hair in my hand, squeezing when he brushes his tongue over my bottom lip.

His breath tickles my ear as his lips move from mine, kissing along my jawline. I gasp as he moves to my neck and deepens his kisses. When he lingers at the base of my throat, a small, breathy moan escapes from me. His hands slide from my thighs to my ass, pulling on the waistband of my panties. He nips at my neck, sending electricity down to my center. I reach for the hem of his shirt and pull it off.

His muscles are tight, waiting, I drag my hand down his chest. Mapping out the lines of his six pack. He suddenly rolls me over to my back, seemingly pulling my underwear down at the same time. He unbuttons his pants and stops.

"Can I have a taste?" He looks at me with a wry smile.

I nod hesitantly. I go to pull off my dress and he stops me. "No, I like it, leave it on." My face flushes with heat. I can't see him but I can feel his lips nipping and kissing up my thighs. I freeze as I can feel his tongue slide down the front of me. His hands grab my ass and pull me in deeper as his tongue dances on my clit. I let out a loud moan. For a moment, my heart speeds up with anxiety as the realization of what he's doing hits me. My mind races through a mental list of things I didn't get a chance to do before this started happening. I didn't get to clean up, or prepare myself, what if he's regretting it. But then, his mouth closes over me and he sucks gently. A full body shiver has me bowing off the bed. His answering groan against my skin wipes every anxious thought from my mind.

I gasp as he slides his fingers into me. I squirm at the pressure.

"Fuck..." Saul says against my inner thigh. "You are so beautiful." He drags his fingers in and out of me and I don't recognize the sounds that I'm making. I feel like I can't breathe around the sensations building in my stomach. "Amber, look at me."

I lift myself up onto my elbows, unable to think enough to be embarrassed or worried about what I look like at this moment. I meet his eyes between my legs, I have no idea if he finds what he's looking for but everything that happens next is completely out of my control. My senses and mind are overthrown by the intoxication of his touch. My legs begin to shake as I dig my hands into his sheets. A pressure I've never felt before builds up in me. His fingers speed up and begin moving as if he's calling something forward in me.

I throw my head back and orgasm hard, I let all the pleasure flow out of me. Moaning loud enough it feels like the house shakes. He comes up from me, pulling my dress over my head, his chest glistening. I unbutton his pants, pull them and his briefs down even though I'm still shaking. His dick bounces out of his pants. Something primal has taken over, I don't even take a moment to examine him before my lips wrap around him.

His cock is hard and skin soft when I pull him deeper. Swirling my tongue around it. My hand steady's the base as I suck. Stroking and feeling his heat along my tongue. He moans loudly, encouraging me to go faster. His hand caresses my cheek, the back of my head, my neck and I shiver.

"Amber, I... Fuuuck.... I want inside... Oh fuck..." He groans.

I happily continue to taste him. His hand slides through my hair, he grips me, pulling gently so I look at him.. He whispers, "please..." His forehead drips with sweat. He pulls me under him, putting one leg between his and hooking the other over his shoulder. I guide him slowly into me. He's thick and the stretch sends euphoric shivers through my body.

"Amber..." He moans as he slides in and out slowly. "You feel so good." His head drops to my shoulder and he places soft kisses against my skin. My body hums against his and I feel like I can't pull in a deep breath around the sensations overwhelming me. Everything is too much and not enough all at once and I don't know what to do.

"Saul." I shiver again as his nose brushes my cheek.

He lifts up just enough to look into my eyes. His eyes are hazy as he looks at me. "What is it?"

"I..." I hunt for the words. "I need," my face flushes as he waits for me to articulate myself. I refuse to let this moment of hesitancy ruin our moment. "I need more."

Saul's mouth crashes into mine, this kiss is all passionate desperation. I pull my knees up around his hips as we both gasp at the change.

His thumb glides down and over my clit, making circles. He begins to plunge deeper and deeper into me. I let out a moan as my hand wraps around his wrist, as I become more and more sensitive. He speeds up and all I can do is groan. He doesn't let up, doesn't change anything, when I look at him there's determination etched into his features. His brows are drawn down as he watches me. It's like he's calculating my reactions and linking them to what he's doing to me. All thoughts leave my brain as I orgasm again, curling in on myself and into his body. Saul seems to catch me, wrapping a hand around the back of my neck, anchoring me to him in a searing kiss.

He grunts, almost like an animal. Thrusting in and out. He pulls out of me, spilling himself all over my stomach. He falls over to his back gasping for air. He whispers a slow 'holy shit' under his breath. He pulls me to his chest and holds me.

"Sorry, we forgot a condom..." Sauls gasps between each word like he can't catch his breath. His eyes are closed and a smile spread across his face. "I've never done it without one." He chuckles. "I understand why men refuse to wear them now."

"It was worth it." I smile, his chest rising and falling.

"It's really only fair since you soaked my sheets." He says, still hunting for air.

"WHAT?" I snap up and see a damp circle on the sheets. "DID I PEE??"

"No? Have you never ejaculated?" He asks unmoving and unphased by the fact I did whatever that is.

"WHAT? I thought that was just a porn thing! Also please don't ever say *ejaculate* again laying naked next to me." My cheeks are flushing.

"It's not, don't think too hard about it, just come back to my arms. It's the technical term," He says breathily, dragging his fingers down my back. I give in all of my energy spent and nestle into his neck. "I love you Amber." He whispers.

"I love you too Saul." I say as I drift off to sleep.

When I wake up I roll over and reach for my purse. Last night was an absolute whirlwind of emotions, and the best sex I've ever had. I think that's what they mean by love making. That makes it sound icky. I pull my purse to the bed with one strap and pull out my phone. It's nearly noon and I have four missed calls.

I roll back over deciding it's best to get back to whoever it is later. When I flop my arm to throw it over Saul he's gone. I pop up and there he is scrolling on his phone on the floor with a pillow, blanket and a flannel set of pjs on. His blanket has pirate anime characters I think I saw on a freshmans bag across it and the pillow is just a giant leaf shaped throw pillow

"What are you doing?" Perplexed by the oddity in front of me.

"Sorry, I couldn't sleep with all of our *cough* fluids on me or the bed. You were sleeping so peacefully so I snuck out, showered, and slept on the floor." He doesn't look at me as he stares at his phone. "Oh, there's a sale on atlas moth caterpillars if I buy them in bulk. My last group kicked the bucket before they could lay." He taps his chins deep in thought about his creepy crawlies.

I smirk, roll my eyes and grab my phone. I pull up my calls and see that Brittany called. I wonder what Andrew told her. I also want to ignore it since I told her not to contact me but she left a voicemail. It won't kill me to listen at least.

"Amber... I'm calling because, because I need my big sister. I..." sobbing ensues. "I'm at Bethton Grove Hope hospital." Each word seemingly needs its own breath. "Andrew left the hospital to go to an interview and is hungover. Mom's mad at me like I had fucking control over this. Like I would fucking ever choose this." I hear a loud groan. A second of silence makes me think the message is over. "I... I just don't want to be alone. Please..."

I don't hesitate, I grab my dress and panties and throw them on. I jog to his bathroom and start fixing my hair and splashing my face with water.

"What's going on?" Saul opens the door slowly, "Is something wrong?"

"I need you to drive me to the hospital like an hour ago." I step past him, grab my purse without pausing and we go straight to his truck. Saul doesn't question or hesitate, he stays in his flannels and puts the truck in gear speeding off to Bethton Grove Methodist Hospital.

Chapter Twenty-Nine

When we arrive I kiss him on the cheek. "I'll give you details later. I love you." Then hop out of the truck. I rush to the emergency room front desk in which an exhausted older woman sits. "Name?" The woman doesn't bother to look up.

"Brittany Brinks? She was brought in this morning." I say stumbling over the 'Brinks part'.

"Room one oh six down the hall to the left." The receptionist still doesn't look at me as she points.

"Thanks." I jog down the hall, the fluorescents burning my eyes.

I could vomit. I have no control, what if this is a lie? My feet slow, but I pick my pace back up. It doesn't matter. I know what it's like to have no one. Until Catherine came along I had no one. I broke my ankle and had no one to call. I had to call a taxi to get back to my apartment. I had never felt so alone.

I turn the corner and spot the room number. A long blue curtain acts as the divider between the hall and the room. I pull open the curtain and see my sister sleeping on her side. An oxygen mask runs from a tank to her face. Her hair is disheveled and she's wearing a classic nineties design hospital gown with the blanket only pulled to her waist. She's hooked up to an IV in her left arm.

She looks awful and pale. My stomach lurches as I spot the blood staining on the blankets. I walk over. She seems so frail and fragile like the forgotten kid from when we were young. I pull up a chair and sit. Watching over her like I always have, releasing I always will.

Her arms are covered in bruises. Her nose is splinted and there's a huge gash through her eyebrow. She looks like she's been in a car wreck. My eyes fill with tears. What the hell happened to my little sister?

"Hello?" A doctor wraps on the frame. He's a tall older Indian man with a hint of a Hindi accent. Brittany doesn't stir. "You must be Amber? She kept asking for Amber."

"Yes... What the hell is going on? I just had a voicemail from her. She didn't sound this bad?" I look down and it feels as if the spot of blood on the blanket grows.

"Brittany signed off for us to share her medical information with you. Right now we are determining if she or the baby needs surgical intervention. She has three broken ribs and a collapsed lung we had to puncture. Her left cheekbone is broken and so is her nose. She has a bruised ovary. The placenta for the baby has a slight tear away from the wall. She has some internal bleeding due to that. But she'll be okay. She's had some morphine so she is out of it." He says with that straight line smile that says sorry in the midwest.

"How? I just don't understand." I say reaching and holding my sister's clammy hand. "How does that even happen?" My heart aches. Everything that's happened doesn't seem to matter anymore.

"Well, she claims she fell down stairs when her husband checked her in…" As he says that she rolls over and the left side of her face is bruised as well. "But you're her family and my experience tells me stairs don't know how to throw a right hook. Her husband also seemed to run off when he dropped her at the door."

The doctor glances at his chart and sighs, "And from what her medical history says this isn't the first set of stairs she's fallen down." He turns to walk away. "I'll be back before shift change, please let her know we can't press charges on stairs."

Anger rages inside me. I can't believe it. I feel sick. I clench my teeth and heat rises from my gut. I see my sister's eyes begin to flicker open. Flashing the icy blue irises she has. Her left though is swirled in red. A smile sprawls across her lips. She rasps a silent "You really came… Is Andrew here?"

"No he's not…" I say holding back tears.

"He…" Tears start flooding her face. "He did this…"

"It's okay, don't worry about that now." I choke back my emotions and try to center myself.

"I don't want to see him." She whispers, closing her eyes.

"You won't have to, not ever again." My voice cracks as tears begin running down my cheeks.

"Promise?" She says between heavy breaths.

"Promise." I brush the hair out of my sister's face as she drifts back off to sleep. I peck her on the head with a kiss. I turned to the doctor. "Did you hear that?"

"Yes." His face is stoic.

"We want to press charges." My voice is monotone to keep it together.

"I called a detective before you even arrived. And security will be placed outside Brittany's door." He turns and exits the room.

"I promise, I will never let him hurt you again." I pull her hand to my face and kiss it. Letting the tears run free.

EPILOGUE

"Do you really want to give birth at Bethton Grove Methodist? I've been researching this thing called a birth center." I tell my little sister.

"Yes I do, Bethton Methodist is literally ten minutes from the Apartment. I'm not driving an hour while in labor to get to that birth center. I am not pushing a baby out on a dashboard." My sister says indignantly from my island. Well, her kitchen island. Brittany has done wonders to this apartment since I moved in with Saul. It looks like one of the apartments you show to get someone to lease. It looks nothing like the pig sty I lived in four months ago.

"But I'm driving and what a great stor-"

"No." Brittany cuts me off. "You are driving my car because I am not getting some weird infection from yours. I saw that weird moldy Meatballs To-go box in the back." She rebuttals. "Plus I want to be comfortable not rushing." Brittany walks around the counter of the island bringing her big swollen belly into view. "What's this really about?"

"I... I don't want you to have him at that hospital... I just see you in that bed even when I drive by." I stutter... We both get silent. Andrew's indictment hearing was a month ago. His Dad made sure he couldn't bond out as punishment. But It was hard for me since he already has been offered a plea deal for aggravated assault instead of attempted murder. I know Brittany wants it all to be over, she doesn't want to think about how he almost killed her, but I want him to pay.

"I'll think about the Birth Center Amb... I guess... I guess..." She starts to cry through her words, "I don't want to think about it so much I pushed that deep down." I reach for her hand and pull her into a hug.

"I don't want it to even pop in your head while you give birth to my favorite person." I reach and rub my sister's bump. "Where's dad?" I redirect the conversation. Our dad moved from Ohio back here when I moved out to stay with Brittany. He is still Dad and has his quirks. Saul thinks he's on the spectrum too. It's weird to have Dad doting on both of us but we've become quite the happy trio.

Our mom milked the situation for her own gain with friends. Fundraising for Brittany but keeping the money. Brittany decided cutting Mom off was the best decision and I can't agree more. It's been a bit of a whirlwind of 'healing' over these past six months.

"Dad is at the Moose lodge setting up for some event." She laughs, "He is such a stereotype of a dad. He even wore sandals with socks in this weather." She gestures to the fall leaves and wind blowing.

My phone dings. I peek and it's a text from Saul.

Saul: Here

"Op, it's time for me to go." I say hugging my little sister. "I love you."

"I love you too, have fun with the no electricity people!" She teases.

"Amish... They are Amish... See if I ever make you a candle again with that attitude." I lean forward and speak to her bump. "You're mom is beautiful but unnecessarily sassy."

Saul has been uncomfortably silent even for him after our breakfast out. I usually can get him to go on at least one endless tangent on the way to the Amish candle making shop, but not today. His fingers dance wildly on the steering wheel and by the furrow in his brow he's over-thinking something. I put my hand on his leg and give a good squeeze. I've learned to be comfortable in silence with Saul. I used to think I had to fill the void but now I can just sit and be near him.

We park at the barn and a familiar face stands waving to us. I slide out of the car and go jogging towards Zakariah. When Saul called this morning to see if we could come make candles Zakariah's wife told us a new calf had been born. Saul said that Zakariah wanted to show me a brand new calf.

"Good Afternoon Miss Amber!" Zakariah says in a drawl.

"Hi Zakariah! Where's my baby cow?" I could jump out of my bright pink rain boots. I'm so excited.

"Oh, he's not in this barn. He's struggling so we separated him." Zakariah states plainly. "He's with Sarah in the red barn we rent out for events."

"Oh... Can I still see him?" I say defeated.

"Of course, he needs a name." Zakariah smirks.

"SHUT UP! Sorry, I mean seriously, can I name him?" I do a tiny clap in excitement.

"Yes mam, have Mr. Saul take you over and the namings all yours." Zakariah smiles.

I turn realizing Saul hasn't even gotten out of the truck and run back yelling my thanks to Zakariah. I get in the door and Saul is still silent.

"Zakariah says the new calf is at the rental barn! AND I CAN NAME HIM!" I squeak out in joy.

Saul starts up the truck, fingers tapping away again. I consider asking but there are some days where he just doesn't talk or talks less. He pulls the truck up to the gravel drive and drives only three minutes down it to the rental barn. I see a few cars at the barn and a few I recognize...

"Saul... Why is Nathan's car here? And my dads?" Saul doesn't look at me but his cheeks flush.

Maybe it's just a coincidence or I know Brittany was looking to host her baby shower somewhere. Maybe here? I took her here a couple months ago with Saul. Saul parks next to another car that looks like a rental.

Saul hops out first and walks around the truck and opens the door helping me out. Still in silence. I'm starting to worry, maybe he feels sick. Or maybe he has bad news to tell me and is scared to. We get to the barn door.

"Are you okay if there is something you need to tell me it's okay." Saul smiles uncomfortably at what I say. But instead of responding he slides open the barn door.

I look in and the place is decorated like a fairy wonderland. Soft acoustic guitar music is being played by my dad sitting off to the right. I look around and see Nathan, Catherine and my little sister holding a camera. There are glittering lights hanging from the ceiling and an arch made of sunflowers. Under the arch is faux grass and a newborn calf with a little bow tie on it.

I can't find words to speak as Saul grabs my hand and walks me to the arch.

"I've been thinking this whole time what I'm going to say..." Sauls fingers dance in mine. "I even googled the last couple nights how-to videos. But how can I describe or say something as special as the person standing in front of me? The person who accepts me no matter my faults. You described yourself as a damsel and distress once and how inconvenient it was. But I want to be the one who rescue's you. I want to be your knight in shining armor everytime. When I am facing the dragon I never face it alone because I have you... and... and..." He begins stuttering, takes a deep breath and unhooks a ring from around the cutest baby calf's neck. Saul kneels to one knee.

"Oh my god..." I whisper.

"Amber, Will you make me the happiest man ever by marrying me." Sauls brown eyes light up and his hesitant smile shows every ounce of fear he has at this moment.

"Yes of course!" I say jumping up and down like a schoolgirl. I put out my left hand and he slides the most stunning ring on my finger. I pull him to his feet and our lips meet. While I feel camera lights flashing around us. All I see is Saul.

"I love you Amber." He says softly on his lips.

"I love you too." I whisper back. I pull back. "Wait, can I still name the calf." I look at the sweet doe eyed animal.

"Oh well yeah." Saul says, smiling the brightest smile I've ever seen.

"I think I'll name him Knight." I turn to the little calf and rub its soft velvet ears.

Our friends rush us and give us the biggest group hug I think I've ever had.